THE RETURN OF
THE SHERIFF

The Return Of The Sheriff

by

Jim Bowden

Dales Large Print Books
Long Preston, North Yorkshire,
BD23 4ND, England.

British Library Cataloguing in Publication Data.

Bowden, Jim
    The return of the sheriff.

    A catalogue record of this book is
    available from the British Library

    ISBN   978-1-84262-642-9 pbk

First published in Great Britain in 1960 by Robert Hale Limited

Copyright © Jim Bowden 1960

Cover illustration © Gordon Crabb by arrangement with
Alison Eldred

The moral right of the author has been asserted

Published in Large Print 2009 by arrangement with
Mr W. D. Spence

Dales Large Print is an imprint of Library Magna Books Ltd.

Printed and bound in Great Britain by
T.J. (International) Ltd., Cornwall, PL28 8RW

PROLOGUE

'Are you goin' to draw or are you jest a low-down yaller coyote?'

The challenging accusation, accompanied by a harsh mocking laugh, tore through Dan McCoy's numbed brain. He clenched his teeth and tightened his lips as his clean cut weather beaten face twitched under the scathing comment.

He did not speak. Nor did he move. His steel blue eyes narrowed as he matched look for look with Wes Brown who stood at the bottom of the four steps leading to the sheriff's office.

Wes glanced at the crowd which had gathered on either side. He grinned.

'Wal, folks, I guess we shore hev a tough sheriff in Red Springs. I reckon you shouldn't be wearin' that thar star if you can't back up those accusations you've been makin' about me and the Circle C boys.'

'I've made no accusations against you, Brown,' answered Dan quietly. 'I don't talk like that. I'd hev come fer you if I'd been

7

goin' to accuse you.'

The young, rugged foreman of the Circle C laughed aloud. 'Wal, here I am.' His smile disappeared in a flash. His dark eyes clouded. 'You'd better back up what you've said about me McCoy. I know you've been wanting to get at me ever since your father crossed my path.'

Dan stiffened. He looked hard at Wes Brown who stood feet astride only a few paces away. At twenty-five he cut a dashing figure in his black outfit. A black vest fitted on top of a black shirt. His black trousers were tucked neatly into boots of the same colour. The black sombrero was set at an angle on his dark hair. Dan watched him carefully. He found himself in the same position as his father who had faced the hard riding tough cowboy two years before on the same spot. In this situation his father had gone for his Colt. He was known to be the fastest on the draw and witnesses said he had drawn first. They couldn't understand why he hadn't pressed the trigger before Wes Brown.

Dan stifled a gasp as he saw a rifle protruding from a window of the Grand Hotel opposite. He controlled the surprise which had almost betrayed his discovery. Now he knew how his father had died! Wes Brown's bullet had hit his father but it hadn't killed him. He was already dead from someone else's bullet. Now he was faced with a similar fate!

The crowd stood silent as the two men faced each other. The townsfolk waited expectantly. Would Dan McCoy share his father's fate? Or was it the end of the road for Wes Brown? In their minds they didn't give Dan a chance. His two years as sheriff had been peaceful but lately he had followed his father's footsteps and had started investigating certain affairs of local ranchers with the result that he found himself in trouble, faced now with a decision which would affect his whole life.

The faces in front of him were a blur, only one stood out – a smiling, mocking face which seemed to say 'I know that you know but you ain't goin' to git proof.' Sweat stood on Dan's face. His brain pounded.

'Draw an' you're a dead man from thet rifle,' he thought. 'Refuse an' you're a coward, your role as sheriff is finished, you'll hev to git right away – far away because reputation, particularly bad ones, hev a habit of followin' you round.'

'Wal Dan McCoy, what's it to be?' shouted

Wes Brown as if sensing Dan's thoughts. His eyes narrowed as he watched the slim cowboy on the sidewalk.

Dan did not speak. He bit his lip as he noticed the ever present rifle. Slowly he turned. Wes rested his hand on the butt of his .45, watching the sheriff carefully. Dan paused, looked hard at the townsfolk of Red Springs. What morbid curiosity made them want to see a gun-fight? Well, they weren't going to see one now. Dan was young, and Dan liked life.

Slowly he walked along the sidewalk, his booted feet splitting the heavy silence with each deliberate step. The urge to turn, to shoot it out was strong, but he saw the rifle following his slow progress.

Suddenly Dan was aware that a dark pretty girl in a flowered gingham frock stood a few paces in front. He stopped. Only last night he had told Barbara Collins how much he loved her; now words choked in his parched throat. He looked appealingly at her, seeking some approval for his decision. Tears filled her dark brown eyes. She tore her gaze away from the young cowboy and slowly turned her back towards him.

Dan trembled at this final branding. The decision was made. He hurried across the wood and as he turned the corner a murmur rose behind him. Dan did not hesitate. He hurried to his home and swiftly put a few belongings together. He had no desire to meet his mother. She would know soon enough and Dan felt he could not face her. Quickly he saddled and bridled his horse, swung into the saddle and without a backward glance left the home he had known since boyhood.

A tall slim cowboy leaned over the bar of Slim's Saloon in the small town of Horse Creek in southern Wyoming. He stared with unseeing eyes at the whisky glass which his long supple fingers encircled.

Behind the counter Slim polished glasses with a stained cloth. The bar was quiet in the early afternoon and Slim watched the stranger carefully, summing him up as lone-wolf, a man who wanted to be left alone. He saw he was a man used to the open and used to drawing his guns which hung low on his hips and were held firm by a thin leather thong tied round his leg. He reckoned the stranger to be about twenty-five, good looking in a rugged way with a kindness in his face which told him that this was no gunman; gunfighter maybe, but only through necessity.

'A grudge,' Slim whispered to himself as he picked up another glass. 'Some trouble the man's fighting out inside himself.'

Slim was a shrewd judge of men and he was not far wrong in his estimation of the weather-beaten, dust-covered cowboy who now stood at his bar. He would have spotted some verification of his judgment had he been able to watch the stranger instead of serving the cowboy who sidled up to the bar.

'Howdy, Shorty.'

'Hi, Slim. Usual fer me.'

Slim slid a glass across the counter and put a bottle in front of the smiling cowboy who poured himself a drink before he spoke again.

'Ever heard of a cowpoke name of Dan McCoy?' he asked casually.

'Dan McCoy?' said the barman thoughtfully stroking his chin. 'Nope, can't say thet I hev.'

'Met a couple of trail riders way back up the Cheyenne Road, wanted to know if I knew a Dan McCoy an' if I'd enquire when I was next in town. Figured he was last heard of in these parts. They'd picked up a message on the trail. Seems this here McCoy's mother is ill down in Texas an'–'

'Thet's it!' Slim slapped his hand on the counter. 'I've got it,' he shouted. 'Thought I'd heard thet name afore. Tale went round thet a McCoy, sheriff of some place down in Texas, I forgit where now, he'd refused to draw – yaller they reckon.'

A splintering crack interrupted his thoughts. He looked sharply at the stranger along the bar. His glass lay shattered in his fingers.

'Sorry,' he muttered quietly, 'must hev gripped it too tightly.'

Slim smiled. 'That's all right.' He moved along the bar to wipe down the counter.

'You'll hev to git tougher glasses,' whispered the stranger.

'Say, you feelin' unwell?' Concern showed in Slim's voice as he noticed the cowboy's face had paled beneath his wind-burnt tan.

'Shore, I'm all right.'

Shorty moved along the bar. 'Couldn't be the shock of hearin' a name could it?' he queried.

'What you mean?' the stranger quirked his eyebrows.

'Wal, are you Dan McCoy by any chance? You're a stranger here an' I jest thought you might be.'

'No, not me,' answered the cowboy,

13

reaching for the glass which Slim had placed in front of him.

With one quick gulp its contents were gone. 'Thanks,' he muttered as he threw a coin on to the counter. He turned sharply and with a quick step strode from the saloon. Slim and Shorty stared at each other, shrugged their shoulders and turned their conversation to other things.

Once outside the tall cowboy quickly untied his horse, climbed into the saddle and left the sleepy town at a steady lope along the south road to Texas.

Chapter 1

Dan McCoy wearily reined his horse to a standstill. The trail sloped gently to Red Springs silhouetted in the gathering darkness. Man and horse stood as one, motionless, tired and exhausted by days of hard riding.

Mud-spattered and dust-stained, soaked by driving rain and dried by the burning sun, Dan had ridden the long trail south towards his native Texas. Always boring into his tortured mind was the fact that he might be too late. The message he had chanced to overhear in that quiet saloon may have been months old. But from the moment he turned from the counter Dan had not hesitated. He never deviated from the purpose of answering that call of a sick mother even though he was returning to a town which had branded him a coward.

McCoy gazed in the direction of the town ahead. Lights were beginning to appear as darkness blanketed the Texas countryside. The travel-stained cowboy turned his gaze to a rocky hillock which lay a few hundred yards to the right of the trail. Memories flowed back to the lonely cowboy. He heeled his horse forward towards the hillock where he had spent many happy boyhood hours with his younger brother, Frank, and pretty Barbara Collins.

Dan paused with his past and glanced towards Red Springs. He had tried to lose his past in some other territory but there was no escape and he knew that some day he would return. Knowing what was inevitable he had practised throwing his Colts until their butts were smooth and he was lightning fast on the draw.

He wheeled his horse back towards the trail and had almost reached it when the sound of hoofs clattering the hard road broke the silence. He drew back into the shadow of a rock, slid from his horse and held his hand over its nostrils. He had no wish to make his presence in Red Springs known just yet. As the riders came nearer they slowed their mounts to a walk. Their shadowy forms rode past and halted a few yards along the road. Dan's hand slid to his Colt, but then he remembered the fork in the road, one trail leading to town, the other to the ranch lands to the south.

'Tomorrow night, then?' said one of the riders.

'Shore. Git the information an' don't be late.'

Dan stiffened as he heard the second cowboy.

There was no mistaking the voice which had mocked him three years ago. Wes Brown still rode the trail!

'You can depend on me. So long.'

'So long.'

The two cowboys spurred their horses into a gallop along different trails.

Dan climbed into the saddle and rode towards Red Springs. Quietly he slipped into town keeping to the shadows. The place had changed little in his absence; a few more houses, another store. He sought out his old home quickly. A light gleamed from a curtained window and another from an upstairs room. He found himself trembling a little as he walked slowly up the path. He reached for the handle of the door, hesitated and then tapped lightly before opening the door and stepping inside closing it quickly behind him.

The girl at the table spun round.

'Dan!' The gasp escaped from her lips in a whisper. Her hands flew to her mouth and the colour drained from her face.

Dan held his finger to his lips signalling her to keep quiet. He crossed the floor in two strides.

'Barbara,' he whispered. 'How – how is she?' The words choked in his mouth dreading the answer he didn't want to hear.

'Weak, Dan, weak, but to see you will do her a power of good. Go to her quickly.' Her voice was gentle with a Texas drawl and as her hand touched his arm Dan suddenly realised how he had yearned for her throughout his wanderings.

For a moment he searched her eyes seeking her feelings for him but he could only see surprise and shock.

Swiftly and silently he mounted the stairs and gently opened the bedroom door.

'Dan!' The whisper filled the room with heart-rending gladness.

'Ma!' Dan stood for a moment and then was on one knee beside the bed. He took the frail hands between his supple fingers and leaned over to kiss his mother gently.

'Dan, you're back.' Tears of joy flowed freely down the sick woman's face.

'Yes, Ma, I'm back – for good,' he added after a moment's pause.

'I knew you would come.' She wiped away

the tears with a small handkerchief and smiled at her son. Then she continued excitedly. 'I've waited for you, Dan, I had to. I feared you would be too late but you're not. You've got to save him, Dan.'

'Sh. Quiet, Ma. It's not good fer you to git worked up. We'll hev plenty of time to talk.'

The grey-haired lady smiled. 'Maybe not as long as you think.'

'Of course, we will,' answered Dan brightly. 'You'll soon be well again an'–'

'You must listen now. You've got to save him. Dan, promise me.'

'Save who ma? What you talkin' about?'

'It's Frank. He's riding with the Circle C. I'm sure Wes Brown is no good and I'm afraid for Frank, he's been seen around a lot lately with Brown.'

Dan stiffened and frowned as trouble clouded his eyes. His mind wandered and then he heard his mother speaking again.

'I see your gun butts are smooth, son. That's good, very good. Guess you'll be a match for Wes Brown now. As good a shot as your Pa used to be, maybe better, eh?' She smiled and patted his hand.

'Shore, I've practised throwin' my guns. I–'

'I always figured you'd return some day,'

Mrs McCoy interrupted, 'and smoke it out with your past. Why did you go away without seeing me?'

'I jest hed to git away, Ma. I knew the town reckoned I was a coward an' I couldn't face you especially after Pa shot it out.'

'Dan, I thought you'd have a good reason. You know that's something I never worked out, how that whipper-snapper name of Wes Brown outdrew your Pa who was so much faster than he was.'

'Wes Brown didn't kill him,' said Dan quietly.

The old lady stared in astonishment.

'What do you mean?'

'Pa was killed by a rifle from the hotel opposite. The same rifle was pointing at me. I saw it an' knew I hadn't a chance so I walked out.'

Mrs McCoy stared at the ceiling. 'So that's how it was done,' she whispered. 'But why?'

'I'd found out a few things an' I reckon Pa had too. We were goin' to be better out of the way.' Dan stood up, hitched up his belt and patted his Colts. 'But I'm back, Ma, an' they'll hev me to reckon with now. Don't worry, Frank will be all right.' He kissed her and left the room.

He found Barbara with Mrs McCoy's

supper tray all ready. As she picked it up she spoke without looking at the travel-stained cowboy.

'I'll fix you something to eat after I've taken this to your mother.'

'Thanks,' Dan muttered. 'I'll jest see to my horse.'

He watched Barbara cross the room before he left the house. He made sure no-one was about before he untied his horse and led it to the stable. Quickly but thoroughly he saw to its needs and made it comfortable. After removing the stains of his long journey Dan felt refreshed as he sat down to enjoy the hot meal which Barbara had prepared for him.

Before he started, Dan spoke. 'Barbara, I want to thank you fer all you've done fer Ma. It shore was mighty kind of you to come over here to stay with her.'

The girl said nothing as she poured out the coffee. The meal proceeded quietly without a word. Dan looked at Barbara, hoping for some smile, some word but the girl kept her eyes downcast. The young cowboy broke the silence with his quiet Texas drawl.

'Barbara, are you glad to see me back?'

Barbara looked up unsmiling. 'Yes, I am. It will do your mother the world of good.'

'Ma, I know; but you – are you glad to see

me back?'

A pretty, troubled face stared at him without speaking. He felt the cold gaze calling him a coward. Suddenly tears filled the dark brown eyes.

'Oh! Dan, why did you do it? Why?' she pleaded. 'I loved you once; it's hard to forget that love.'

'I've never forgotten it. It's been with me on the trail always, punchin' cattle, ridin' the stage, trail herdin', wherever I've been, whatever I've done I've never forgotten you. Despair came deep at times and it was only the memory of you that kept me goin'. When I left Red Springs I was mad against everyone. I headed north an' in Clay County, Missouri, I almost joined the James gang; thought I'd bring them down here an' teach this here town a lesson. Then I thought of you. I knew I'd come back some day an' I didn't want to return to you as an outlaw.' Dan paused, looked longingly at the girl. 'Barbara, I love you still.'

'Sh. Sh. You mustn't say that,' Barbara whispered.

Dan took her soft white hand. 'But why?' He put her hand against his lips. For a brief moment she let it rest there then she quickly pulled it away.

'Don't, Dan, don't. It will only make it worse.' Barbara turned from the table.

'What's the matter, Barbara? Can't we pick it up where we left off?' Dan pleaded.

'It's not as easy as that, Dan. You see I'm to be married to Luke Fennell in two weeks!'

Dan gasped. He jumped from the chair, sending it spinning across the floor.

'What! Luke Fennell! Who's he?'

'Followed you as sheriff,' answered the girl.

'But why–'

Barbara turned on him sharply, accusation in her voice. 'What did you expect me to do, Dan? What could I do after what I saw? What could I think? You left without an explanation, without a word. Nobody knew where you had gone. Dan, I couldn't wait all my life in the hope that some day you would return. If only you had come sooner.'

Dan stared at her. He knew she was right and wondered why he had expected her to wait for him – she couldn't know he intended to return some day.

'You turned your back on me; branded me like the rest. In my fury I naturally left as soon as I could. But afterwards I forgave you – you couldn't know what I knew and

23

why I didn't draw that afternoon.'

'Why didn't you shoot it out with Wes Brown?' Barbara asked hoarsely.

Before Dan could answer the door opened and a young neatly dressed cowboy stepped inside. The smile slipped from his face when he saw Dan. His eyes narrowed smouldering with a quick jealousy.

Barbara brushed away her tears. 'Hello, Luke,' she said trying hard to smile. 'Come in, this is Dan McCoy; he has come–'

A sneer crossed the newcomer's face. 'So this is the celebrated McCoy. I've no wish to meet a coward and I'd rather–'

Dan sprang across the table smashing the words in Luke Fennell's mouth and sending him sprawling on the floor. His hand moved towards his .45 but Dan's Colt had leaped into his hand and Fennell found himself looking up into a cold muzzle.

'I wouldn't touch thet if I were you,' drawled Dan. 'Now git up an' git out an' don't ever come here again.'

Slowly and sullenly the cowboy climbed to his feet. He picked up his Stetson and glared angrily at Dan as he wiped away the trickle of blood from his mouth with the back of his hand.

'I'll git even with you fer this, McCoy,' he

hissed. He turned for the door but glanced back at Barbara. 'I'll see you at home an' the less you hev to do with the fellow the better I'll like it.'

'Barbara will please herself.' Dan's voice was cold. 'Now git.'

Luke rammed his Stetson on his head, turned sharply and strode from the house. Dan moved to the window and watched Fennell's shadowy form mount his horse and ride away. He was puzzled. He felt sure he had heard that voice before. He slipped his Colt back into its holster and turned to face Barbara.

'I'm sorry I had to do thet,' he apologised.

'You were right, Dan. I'm sorry Luke acted like that. He had no right to—'

'Don't worry about it, Babs.'

'Everyone will know you're back in town, Dan.' Concern showed on Barbara's face.

'Can't be helped.' Dan shrugged his shoulders as he sat at the table. 'Any more coffee, please?'

As Barbara poured the coffee, Dan's mind was searching for a voice. Suddenly he slapped the table.

'Got it!' he shouted. 'Luke was with Wes Brown at the fork in the road near our hillock!'

Chapter 2

Before Barbara could question Dan's remark a knock came from upstairs. Barbara hurried to answer and when she returned the cowboy was thoughtfully sipping another cup of coffee.

She entered the room slowly and did not speak until she sat down beside Dan.

'I'm sorry for what I did three years ago,' she said laying her hand on his arm. 'Your mother has just told me what happened.' She paused but Dan did not speak. 'I don't understand it, Dan. Why should anyone want to kill you?'

The young cowboy put down his cup and turned to the girl he had once hoped to marry.

'I'm glad you know, Babs. I was goin' to tell you but Luke Fennell comin' here interrupted me.' A sadness crept into his eyes as he looked hard at the pretty girl. Suddenly he blurted out, 'Must you marry him? I still love you.'

'Dan,' she answered quietly, 'everything is

arranged. I–'

'He's no good,' answered Dan, his voice cold as he emphasised the words.

The girl was startled by the forthright condemnation. Her eyes were troubled.

'You've no right to say that. You don't know him,' she protested somewhat weakly.

'He was with Wes Brown tonight.'

'What's that got to do with it? You can't condemn a man for being with Wes. Your brother rides with the Circle C bunch.'

'So Ma tells me,' drawled the cowboy, 'an' he'll be in trouble unless I can save him quick.'

'What have you got on Wes Brown?' A puzzled frown marked the pretty forehead.

For a moment Dan did not speak. He leaned forward on the table and in an earnest voice he told Barbara of his suspicions.

'I had nothin' definite on him but as you'll hev guessed, with a rifle planted in the hotel, it was a planned job when he came gunnin' fer me. He was scared of what I might know. I guess Pa must hev hed his suspicions too although I didn't know it at the time.' He paused thoughtfully. 'You see, Babs, I figured Wes Brown was behind the rustlin' which had been goin' on around here.'

Barbara gasped. 'Wes Brown!'

Dan nodded. 'I was only suspicious but the fact thet he tried to kill me seems to confirm my ideas. Has the rustlin' continued since I left?'

'For a little while, then it stopped but for over a year now cattle have been rustled again. You can't think that Luke has anything to do with it merely because you thought he was with Wes Brown tonight. Why, you don't even know if it really was him.'

'No, but the voices were the same. I'm shore of thet.'

'But he's curbed the rustling and it's never been on the same scale as it was before Luke came. Everyone says its because we have a tough sheriff and you'll find the cattlemen think highly of him.'

Dan smiled. 'This could all be part of the game.'

'But why?'

'To git him in favour an' gain the confidence of the folks around here. The ranchers might even tell him about plans so's he could give them protection – an ideal situation if you want to rustle cattle.'

'Yes, but the Circle C's lost cattle as well.'

'Again, it could be done to divert suspicion. The steers are never seen again; all trace of them disappears so it would be easy to rustle your own cattle or at least your boss's cattle.'

'Then you suspect Wes Brown as the ring leader.'

'Wal, I'm not shore on thet score. He has the ideal opportunity especially as his boss spends a great deal of time on his other spread further south. But I've wondered at times if Wes has the brains to rustle on a big scale an' remember it was being done in a big way three years ago. Things may hev quietened down but you don't say thet Luke has made any arrests. I figure if the rustlers are still at large then there'll be bigger raids ahead.' He paused a moment before he added, 'Babs, I aim to find out, save Frank an' show I was no coward three years ago.'

'Be careful, Dan,' the girl pleaded.

Dan smiled. 'An' I aim to do it before your weddin'. I figure I'm right about Luke an' I don't want you makin' a fool of yourself by marryin' a crooked lawman.' He pushed himself from the table. 'Wal, I guess I'll turn in, Babs, an' forget it all until tomorrow.'

Dan settled down for the night but in spite of his wearying ride sleep came slowly as his mind was occupied with thoughts of Luke Fennell.

At that moment Luke Fennell was riding hard towards the south. He quirked his horse angrily as he smarted under the recollection of his treatment at the hands of Dan McCoy. He rubbed his chin, still sore from the blow, and swore revenge as he flattened himself in the saddle and urged his horse faster. Rounding a small hill he saw the lights shining from the Circle C ranch. Soon he was sliding his horse to a stand-still outside the foreman's cabin. He hurled himself from his horse and burst through the door.

'What the–?' gasped a surprised Wes Brown leaping from his bunk.

Fennell slammed the door behind him.

'Dan McCoy's back!' he panted.

The foreman of the Circle C stared at the sheriff in amazement but suddenly the surprise vanished from his face and he started to laugh. 'You ridden all this way jest to tell me thet? You must be loco.'

'But it's McCoy!' shouted Luke.

'So what?' mocked Brown.

Fennell, taken aback at the way Brown had received the news, sank on to a chair.

'Wal, from what you told me, this McCoy was on to you, so he can make trouble now.'

'You didn't see him when he faced me

30

three years ago. Scared stiff he was. He won't make trouble.' The foreman shook some tobacco from his sack and rolled himself a cigarette.

'You ain't seen this new McCoy,' snapped Luke. 'I felt his fist when I called fer Barbara, and–'

Brown laughed. 'Thet's your fault, Luke. You could hev out drawn him, he wasn't fast with a gun.'

'Thet's what you think,' snarled the sheriff, 'I tried it an' found a man thet's lightnin' fast.'

The Circle C foreman paused as he was about to light his cigarette. This news surprised him because he knew Luke Fennell was handy with a gun. Wes shrugged his shoulders.

'Wal, the fact thet he's here may mean nothin'. I guess he's probably come to see his Ma. Besides if he did make trouble we hev a trump card – ain't we got his kid brother ridin' fer us?'

Luke's face showed relief at the implication. 'Shore. You're smart, Wes, but he's never rustled with us so you'd better hev him on the job mighty quick.'

'Naturally. It'll be the next one an' you'll hear about thet tomorrow night. Now git

31

yourself back to Red Springs an' act natural like an' don't let McCoy see you with me.'

Luke pushed himself off the chair. As he turned for the door Wes stopped him. 'Forgit McCoy, I'll handle him if necessary. Jest play your part an' everythin' will be all right. Don't be late tomorrow night an' be shore to confirm thet information.'

'Shore,' answered Luke. 'Do I git to meet the boss tomorrow?'

'He wants things kept jest as they are,' smiled Wes.

'Who is he?' queried Luke pulling his Stetson on to his head.

Wes drew deep on his cigarette and blew a long cloud of smoke into the air. He regarded the sheriff with cold eyes. 'Been figurin'?' he asked.

'Wal,' drawled Fennell, 'could be anyone around here; could be your boss, Hiram Griffiths. It could even be you,' he added quietly.

The two cowboys stared at each other. Brown did not speak. His eyes narrowed slowly. Fennell averted his gaze and as soon as he did so the foreman hissed so viciously that the sheriff was startled. 'You've got a nice set up, Fennell, with a nice come-back in cash. If I was you I wouldn't git curious, you're liable to git hurt if you do.'

Fennell stood for a second then swung on his heel and left the hut.

Chapter 3

Dan McCoy was up early the following morning to find that Barbara was already downstairs and had an appetising breakfast ready for him. Travel weariness had vanished after his early night and sound sleep.

'I aim to be out most of the day,' he told Barbara. 'Probably be back around mid-afternoon.'

He fastened his belt and checked the hang of his holsters. After tying them to his leg to hold them firm his hands flew to his guns and whipped them out in front of a startled Barbara.

'Sorry.' Dan grinned apologetically as he slipped the Colts back into their holsters. 'Guess it's habit – practisin' I mean.'

Barbara smiled back. 'I wish you hadn't to use them,' she said.

The cowboy picked up his Stetson, shouted goodbye to his mother and turned to the door. Barbara stopped him before he opened it. 'Dan do be careful,' she whispered. Her brown eyes gazed at the handsome weather-beaten face. Reaching upwards she kissed him lightly on the cheek, turned and hurried upstairs before Dan could speak.

He gazed after the slim figure, his heart pounding from the gentle touch of her soft lips. He pulled on his Stetson and left the house deep in thought. He soon had his horse ready for the trail and as he left the stable Dan swung into the saddle. He turned into the dusty road and looked back to see Barbara waving goodbye from the upstairs window. Dan smiled, urged his horse into a steady trot and headed towards the ranch-lands south west of Red Springs. This road kept him out of the main street and he saw no-one as he left the town.

He covered the miles steadily and was delighted to be back in familiar country again. He knew these ranges and their owners well. Herds of cattle fed on the rolling grass land and he estimated their numbers and condition, storing the information in his mind for he knew this might prove of value in the future. He reckoned Zeke Gordon's herd had grown half as big again over the past three years whereas Jake Richard's herd was about the same size. He was careful not to make contact with anyone and although he saw several cowboys on the ranges and knew they had seen him he kept well away.

Towards mid-day Dan sent his horse to the top of a ridge which overlooked John Wayman's ranch. A hard, tough man, who had fought for his rights in the early days of the West, Wayman had sought peace in Texas. He had built up a large herd of fine cattle but had suffered at the hands of the rustlers shortly before Dan had left Red Springs. His land adjoined the Circle C and Dan recalled that John Wayman had almost sold out to the boss of the Circle C after this set-back. At the last minute he had changed his mind and had set about rebuilding his herd. As his horse twisted its way through the scrub to the top of the ridge Dan wondered just how successful John Wayman had been. At the top of the rise the lone cowboy pulled his horse to a stop. For a moment he gazed around him at the rich grass land through which the Brazo river wound its way. He swung out of the saddle and left his horse loose to champ the tufts of grass and scrub.

He walked across the ridge to a huge flat stone, sat down, pushed his Stetson to the back of his head and rolled himself a cigarette. After the first long draw Dan turned his gaze towards Wayman's ranch house. Smoke curled lazily from the chimney and Dan noticed a number of saddled horses standing near the bunk house. Three cowboys were carrying goods into a chuck wagon and there was an air of activity about the place. Dan's eyes wandered across the countryside searching for Wayman's cattle. A cloud of dust rose some miles away and Dan reckoned that there must be a sizeable herd somewhere on the range. With much activity on the ranch he figured that some big movement was impending within the next twenty-four hours. He had been part of similar operations when he had been working cattle in Montana. He figured that John Wayman had wasted no time in getting back into the market and in all probability would move his herd to the rail head at Wichita Falls the following day. Dan determined to take a closer look to add confirmation to his theories.

He was about to whistle for his horse when he noticed two figures emerge from the ranch house. They paused for a moment, then shook hands before one of them walked down the steps, unhitched his horse and swung into the saddle. The rider moved slowly through the line of cottonwoods to the road before turning his horse in the direction of Red Springs. Realising that this would bring the cowboy below the ridge Dan decided to wait before he moved nearer the ranch. He slipped off the rock and lay flat along the edge of the ridge keeping out of sight yet commanding a full view of the road. Slowly the rider drew nearer. Dan strained his eyes to see if he could recognise him. The cowboy was not in a hurry and his mount plodded the dusty road at a steady walk. Suddenly Dan gasped. 'Luke Fennell!' he whispered to himself. 'Now what brought you out here?' Dan, his brow knitted in a puzzled frown, watched the sheriff pass below his vantage point.

Once the rider was out of sight behind the ridge Dan jumped to his feet and hurried to his horse. He gathered the reins and leaped into the saddle urging his horse to the edge of the ridge. The animal slipped and slithered sending little showers of stones tumbling in front as it twisted down the narrow path to the grass land below.

Dan decided to make himself known to John Wayman. He had been very friendly with his father and Dan felt sure he would welcome him. Maybe he would learn why Luke Fennell had visited the ranch before

what Dan guessed was an important movement of cattle.

The cowboy sent his horse at a trot along
the road towards the ranch. He turned
through the line of trees and slowed to a
walk as he approached the house. Buildings
and fences were in a state of good repair and
the ranch itself bore signs of prosperity.

'Old man Wayman's shore done well for
himself,' mused Dan.

He halted his horse in front of the house
and swung out of the saddle. As his feet
touched the ground he heard a door shut
and the footsteps on the wood suddenly
stop. Dan turned sharply to find himself
staring into the cold muzzle of a .45.

'Keep your hands away from your irons,
boy.' The voice was keep and quiet but full
of determination.

'I'd be a fool to go fer 'em with thet facin'
me, Mr Wayman,' said Dan quietly.

John Wayman's eyes narrowed. 'What you
want McCoy?' he drawled. 'You're not
welcome here so you can git as far as thet
hoss can carry you.'

'Now wait a minute, Mr Wayman–'

'I've no time to waste on yella bellied
coyotes like you. I may hev been a friend of
your Pa but his son's no friend of mine. The

sooner you're out of my sight the better I'll like it.'

Dan smarted under the insults but he kept control of his feelings. He knew why John Wayman had succeeded. Wayman was one of the old pioneering breed, full of determination, and hard work and prepared to go through anything to succeed. Dan admired him but he saw the work and worry of restarting his ranch had left its mark. Wayman's face was older and more lined than when Dan last saw him. His hair greying at the temples was a little thinner but the young cowboy realised that the outdoor life had kept the rancher fit and active and Dan realised that he was still a man to be reckoned with.

'Wal, are you goin' or hev I to hev you thrown off this ranch?'

Dan did not move. He decided not to waste words and came straight to the point. 'I reckon you are goin' to move some cattle, Mr Wayman. Why was Luke Fennell here?'

Wayman was startled by the question. A puzzled frown creased his forehead. He stared curiously at Dan. 'What you want to know fer?'

'I'm kinda interested,' replied Dan.

'In Luke Fennell or my cattle?'

'Both.'

Wayman did not answer for a moment. Strange thoughts and new suspicions flashed into his mind as he stared at the ex-sheriff.

'*You* could have rustled them cattle three years ago I suppose,' he muttered.

Dan gasped. He realised that he had roused suspicions in the older man's mind. Anger flared in his face.

'I did not,' he hissed between tight lips. His knuckles showed white as he clenched his fists.

'Be thet as it may you needn't expect to rustle this herd. Sheriff Fennell's providin' protection which is more than you did when you were sheriff. He's kept the rustlers reasonably quiet. It shore was a good day fer Red Springs when you decided to be a coward.' Wayman laughed grimly. 'Funny how things work out.' His grin disappeared. 'A pity you didn't choose to walk out a couple of weeks sooner then maybe Fennell would hev saved thet herd you should hev protected. Now git. You're dirt around here.'

Dan was shaken by the accusations of the older man. He had never realised that anyone would blame him for the rustlings. He saw how well Brown and Fennell had played this game so that Wayman hated the ex-sheriff and trusted the present lawman.

McCoy was about to speak but suddenly he changed his mind, turned, climbed into the saddle and without a word pulled his horse round and left the ranch at a trot.

The rancher watched him go, shook his head as he replaced his .45 in its holster and headed for the chuck wagon.

Once out of sight of the house Dan swung his horse towards the south-east in the direction of the cloud of dust which he had observed from the top of the hill. He kicked his broad-chested mount into a gallop and with long powerful strides it quickly covered the miles across the grass land. He followed an old trail alongside the river then turned and climbed steadily for about two miles. The trail flattened across some scrubland and then dropped into a wide shallow valley.

Dan pulled his horse to a halt. Lush grass stretched along the valley which lay between two stretches of rounded hills. The low moan of cattle rose and fell from the herd of longhorns about a mile away. Dan estimated that there were about six thousand head of cattle and more were being brought in by cowboys who skilfully twisted and turned their horses to keep the steers in compact bunches moving towards the main herd.

'John Wayman is shore goin' to make some cash with that lot,' thought Dan. 'What a haul fer the rustlers. Git these an' Wayman's broke. He'd hev to sell out.'

Dan pulled his horse round and heeled it into a steady lope towards Red Springs.

Chapter 4

It was shortly after noon when Dan's horse
flicked up the dust of the main street in Red
Springs. He headed for the saloon to slake
his parched throat before returning home to
clean up.

He rode slowly past the houses on the
outskirts of the town and held to the centre
of the road as he passed the false-fronted
buildings. The street was quiet under a hot
sun but here and there a few cowboys
lounged against the rails of the sidewalk.
They paid little attention to the dusty
cowboy and Dan cast them a cursory glance
as he rode on. He recognised no-one. Several
cowboys lounged in wicker chairs in the
shade of the balcony of the town's only hotel.
Dan's eyes sharpened when he saw one of
them sit upright and stare in his direction. He
smiled at the look of surprise on old Clint
Schofield's face.

Clint had changed little during the past
three years. He was a shrewd, wise man now
in his middle-fifties and had served as deputy

sheriff to Dan and to his father before him. Dan quirked his eyebrows when he realised that a star no longer hung on Clint's shirt. His puzzled frown changed to a smile when Clint's lined face leaned towards the cowboy next to him. The cowboy looked in Dan's direction and then muttered to the occupant of the next chair. So the word went down the line until seven men roused from their sleepy lolling were sitting upright staring at Dan as he halted his horse in front of them. Dan leaned forward resting his hands on his saddle.

'What's wrong?' he grinned. 'You all look as if you've seen a ghost.'

For a moment no-one spoke.

'Well – er – we hev, sorta,' stammered the wide-eyed Clint.

'Meanin' me?' laughed Dan.

'Well – er – shore,' gasped the older man.

'Never expected to see you back here,' drawled a dark, long-faced man whom Dan recognised as Zeke Gordon.

'Guess you've come back to see your Ma,' said another.

'Yep, an' fer other reasons,' answered Dan.

'Such as?' queried Clint. Dan saw a gleam spring into the old deputy's eyes. He rea-lised that Clint hoped that he had returned to redeem himself and he knew that he could count on Clint as a friend. But this pleasing thought was spoiled by the remarks of the older townsfolk.

'Reckon if I was you I'd blow, McCoy. We ain't fergitten thet Red Springs once hed a coward fer a sheriff. We're ashamed of thet an' less we see of you to remind us of it the better we'll like it.'

Clint jumped to his feet. 'Now see here,' he protested but before he could say any more the speaker continued.

'An' from what I hear you may hev been rustler too. Zeke, you'd better watch them cattle of yours.'

Dan stared at the speaker for a moment, whilst Clint spluttered for words, but he ignored the insulting remarks and turned his horse to the saloon across the street.

He climbed from the saddle and hitched his horse to the rail in front of the saloon. Dan paused in front of the batwings and swiftly surveyed the smoke-filled room. About twenty cowboys were gambling and drinking at various tables, whilst another four propped up the bar. As he pushed open the batwings Dan took careful note of a group of six hard-faced cow-punchers seated together. Their clothes were dust covered and Dan reckoned that they had reached town just a short time ahead of himself. They gave him little attention as he strode across to the bar but by the whisperings in other places he guessed he'd been recognised. He sidled up to the counter, rested one boot on the foot rail and leaned his elbows on the polished counter. He flicked his sombrero off his forehead.

'Hello, Blackie,' he drawled, grinning at the dark, swarthy bartender who paused in his polishing when he saw Dan.

'Howdy, McCoy.' Surprise showed in Blackie's voice but he made no further comment. 'What can I git you?' he asked.

'A beer, please. It's shore dry work ridin' today.'

Dan glanced in the mirror which covered the wall behind the bar and saw Clint Schofield look round the room as he stepped through the batwings.

'Better make it two,' Dan instructed Blackie as he saw Clint move in his direction.

'Say, Dan,' Clint panted as he joined the ex-sheriff, 'I want to apologise fer the reception you got out there.' He jerked his head in the direction of the street.

'Fergit it,' answered Dan shrugging his shoulders.

'You can't really blame folks fer thinkin' the way they do after you walked out. I knew you were on to somethin' but could never forgive you backin' down in front of Wes Brown. Wust thing you could hev done.'

'Clint,' Dan lowered his voice, 'I was on to somethin' an' I hed my reasons fer what I did.'

An excited gleam came into the older man's eyes. 'I knew it,' he said slapping the counter. 'I allus said you weren't yalla.'

Dan glanced swiftly round. 'Quiet,' he said, 'I'm here visitin' Ma really. Come round there after I leave here.'

'Shore will, son. Reckon I'll fix on my old gun belt agin.'

'Might be wise,' muttered Dan picking up his glass.

Footsteps clattered on the wooden sidewalk; the batwings creaked as they were hurled open and Clint saw Dan stiffen. He followed Dan's gaze into the mirror and saw four cowboys crossing the floor led by one dressed in black.

'Wes Brown!' muttered Dan.

Clint glanced sharply at his companion whose face had paled a little. His eyes narrowed as he watched the newcomers in the mirror but his eyes were no longer on

48

Wes Brown, instead they watched the youngster behind him.

'Frank!' he whispered.

'Five beers over here, Blackie,' shouted Wes as they joined the six cowboys whom Dan had observed when he entered the saloon.

Blackie shot a glance at Dan but made no comment. Clint watched Dan carefully. He could almost feel the tension which gripped the ex-sheriff as he watched his brother in the company of the cowboy from whom he had backed down three years ago.

Dan saw that Frank was no longer the kid brother he had known. The cowboy he saw now was a grown man, tall, broad-shouldered with clean cut features, and packing two guns.

Suddenly Dan picked up his glass and drained its contents. Clint looked at him with alarm.

'Careful what you do, Dan,' he whispered as Dan tested the hang of his Colts.

'It'll be all right,' answered Dan quietly. 'I only want Frank away from thet bunch.'

'There's too many of 'em,' said Clint, 'an' Wes Brown'll stand no nonsense especially when he's got thet lot with him.'

Dan smiled but said nothing. As soon as he

saw that Blackie had served the drinks he turned and walked slowly towards the Circle C bunch. The cowboys were so engrossed in their talk that they did not notice Dan until he was standing close to the table. The conversation stopped and eleven men stared at the ex-sheriff.

'Howdy, Frank.' Dan's face was expressionless as he greeted his brother and ignored the others.

The younger McCoy stared in amazement. 'Dan!' The word caught in his throat before it became a long drawn out whisper.

Wes Brown tilted his chair on its back legs and carefully rolled a cigarette. He glanced casually at Dan and showed such little surprise that Dan was certain that he already knew he had returned to Red Springs.

'Wal, if it ain't old yaller McCoy,' he mocked.

Dan did not move a muscle and ignored the remark.

'I'm glad to see you Frank; come over an' hev a drink with me,' he said.

Frank glanced round the Circle C cowboys and then at his foreman. Brown, his face broken by a faint smile, continued to roll his cigarette. Frank looked at his elder brother.

'Well I – er – I–'

Wes Brown let his chair slip forward with a crash on its two front legs. At the same time he leaned forward resting his arms on the table.

'Truth of the matter is,' he drawled, 'I don't like my men associating with yaller coyotes so he'd better sit where he is.'

Dan's eyes narrowed. 'My brother can please himself who he speaks to.'

'Not so long as he rides with me,' answered Brown. 'Besides I shouldn't think he'd hev anythin' to do with you; he hed a helluva life fer a while after you walked out. Be a man an' tell him, Frank.'

Dan looked at his brother whose face had paled. Frank clenched his teeth, the memory of three weeks following Dan's departure forced themselves upon him.

'Wes is right,' he hissed. Now the initial shock of seeing his brother was over anger and disgust began to come into his voice. 'You'd better git out of here. I want nothin' to do with you. You bein' here will only revive the past. I–'

'You bet it will!' Anger rose in Dan's voice. 'Frank you're ridin' with a no good bunch. Come with me an' you'll learn the truth.'

'Wes was kind to me after you'd gone; he gave me this job an'–'

'He'll hev done it fer a purpose,' snapped Dan.

'I'm O.K. with the Circle C.' Frank spoke with a tremor. 'At least they've no yaller streaks amongst them. You ain't fit to be your father's son!'

The words cut deep into Dan. Colour drained from his face; he bit hard on his lips; his eyes smouldered with anger. But what else could he expect his brother to say? He had left without an explanation and no doubt Wes Brown had expressed his own opinions.

The saloon went deathly quiet. Cowboys stopped talking; gamblers stopped playing and drinkers slowly put down their glasses. No one spoke to another man like this and got away with it, brother or not. All eyes turned on Dan.

He choked back the retorts which sprang to his lips and said quietly, 'You comin', Frank?'

Before Frank could speak Wes pushed himself off the chair. 'You heard your brother McCoy. Now if you know what's good fer you you'll high-tail it out of here.' His voice was quiet but assertive.

The two cowboys faced each other matching look for look. No-one in the saloon moved. Wes Brown was cool, confident, certain of the outcome. To him it was as if three years had never been and he was facing the same Dan McCoy but to the ex-sheriff things had changed. He was more certain of himself, he was faster on the draw and no rifle covered his move.

'I'm takin' Frank with me,' he said coldly.

'You're not,' replied Brown as he went for his Colt but before the gun was half way out of its holster he found himself staring into the round hole of two cold .45s. He gaped with amazement, his hand frozen in the middle of the draw.

'Surprised?' smiled Dan. Quickly the grin vanished. 'Jest leave thet gun an' unbuckle your belt. Thet goes fer the rest of you; git on your feet.'

Reluctantly the Circle C bunch climbed to their feet. Dan watched them carefully, his eyes like cold blue steel. Slowly the cowboys fumbled with their belts. A movement to his left caught Dan's eye. Like a flash of lightning he turned his .45 and almost before the chisel-faced cowboy touched his gun it was blown from his hand. Smoke drifted slowly across the room.

'Thet shore was mighty stupid of you,' he said quietly to the man who nursed his damaged hand. 'Don't anyone else try it,' he hissed grimly. 'I might not be so lenient next time. Now, move, quick. An' back up to thet wall.' Gun belts clattered to the floor and the ten cowboys shuffled backwards scowling at Dan.

'O.K. Frank, now come with me.'

The younger brother hesitated but seeing the determined look in Dan's eyes he stepped forward. Dan backed slowly towards the batwings. He had almost reached them when a faint squeak indicated that they were being opened gently. But he had heard the noise too late. Before he could turn he felt a muzzle pressed into his back.

'All right, drop 'em.'

Dan's guns clattered to the floor and he was pushed savagely forward. Grinning cowpokes shouted as they picked up their gun belts and refastened them round their hips. Wes laughed as he stepped forward.

'Didn't expect to git away with it, did you McCoy even if you had got outside? Nice work Russ.'

'Heard the shot, boss, an' spotted this coyote through the window.'

Wes nodded his approval then turned to two of his riders. His voice was low and guarded as he spoke. The conversation was brief and after a word to Frank three of them left the saloon. As the batwings swung behind them Brown turned to Dan.

'Your brother wants nothin' to do with you so you'd better keep away from him. In fact it'd be better if you hit the trail away from Red Springs and the Brazo country. I think some of my boys would like to give you a bit of advice on this; wouldn't you?'

A murmur of approval ran through the Circle C riders as they grinned at each other.

'Right boys I think four of you's sufficient to see Mr McCoy onto the north trail.'

Dan paled as he saw Brown pick out the four biggest roughnecks in the bunch.

A burly, evil-faced, stubble-chinned cowboy who had been addressed as Butch drew his Colt and stepped forward.

'Right, Mr ex-sheriff, you can march,' he snarled pushing Dan roughly towards the door.

Dan staggered, tripped over a chair and sprawled on the floor. As he picked himself up he saw Clint start as if about to help him but Dan's eyes flashed a warning and Clint did not interfere. The four cowpokes closed in on Dan.

'Hold it!' Wes halted them. He picked up

Dan's Colts, emptied the chambers and threw the guns to one of the cowboys. 'Here Al,' he called. 'He might want 'em when he rides north. A word of warnin' McCoy,' continued Brown smoothly. 'When these four hev finished with you don't return, we may not give you another chance next time.' He turned to the bar. 'Set 'em up, Blackie,' he shouted.

Strong hands gripped Dan's arms and with a propelling heave sent him through the batwings, tumbling across the board-walk, to sprawl in the dust. Anger flared when he heard the laughter in the saloon and he realised he could do nothing when he struggled to his feet to find the four roughnecks standing over him.

'Now git on your hoss,' snarled Butch.

Dan glanced at the four grim faces, evil shone in their eyes and Dan knew he would be worse off when he left them. He stumbled to his horse and climbed into the saddle. He was tempted to try to make a dash to escape but realised it would be useless. As he turned his horse on the dusty street Dan saw Clint leave the saloon, pause for a moment before hurrying across the street. A cowboy closed in on either side and Butch and Al dropped in behind. The grim procession headed along the north road out of town.

The young cowboy's mind fought to find some means of escape; his eyes searched for something to help him to outwit these four no-good characters, but all to no avail. They rode slowly. The roughnecks had obviously done this before and realised that the longer the ride was prolonged the more their victim was tortured with the thoughts of what was going to happen. But they underestimated Dan for the slower the ride the more chance he saw to escape; he felt sure Clint would do something to help him. Dan kept on the alert although to the other riders he looked worried about his fate.

'We've come 'bout four miles, Butch, ain't that far enough?' questioned the cowpoke riding on Dan's right, eager to get on with the part of the job he liked.

'Naw,' laughed Butch, 'Jest look at the yeller streak, scared stiff he is, let him taste the agony a bit longer.'

The four riders laughed loudly and rode steadily along the trail.

'Don't worry, McCoy,' shouted the other rider good-humouredly as he slapped Dan on the back with such force that he sprawled on the horse's neck.

Dan smiled grimly to himself. He had gained a few precious minutes by his act. His eyes pried into every available cover hoping help would be forthcoming but all was still under the blazing sun.

They rode a further mile before Butch called a halt. 'In those trees,' he called, indicating a small wood a few yards from the road.

Butch and Al swung out of their saddles but the other two remained mounted alongside Dan watching him carefully. The young cowboy looked round desperately but saw no hope of escape.

'All right, McCoy, git down,' snapped Butch. 'This is where we teach you a thing or two thet you ain't likely to forgit in a hurry.'

Dan did not move. Suddenly the two cowpokes on either side grabbed him and flung him from the saddle.

'You heard Butch,' snarled one as Dan hit the hard trail.

Al grabbed Dan by the shirt, dragged him roughly to his feet and smashed his huge hairy fist into his face sending him reeling across the road. The four cowboys leaped towards Dan and before he could move lifted him bodily and walked towards the trees.

'A bit cooler in the shade,' laughed Butch as they dropped Dan unceremoniously on the ground. Like a flash Dan twisted and jumped to his feet. Before the roughnecks realised what was happening Dan had crashed his fist into one of their faces staggering him against a tree and had kicked another's feet from under him. He was determined to give a good account of himself before he went down under their blows. He spun round to face Butch and Al who rushed towards him. Dan's solid fist pulped Al's nose and as Butch's huge arms encircled him he drove his knee sharply into Butch's groin. He yelled with pain but hung grimly to Dan as they spun to the ground. Over and over they rolled each struggling to come out on top. Dan's fist crashed against Butch's sharp teeth but before he could do any more damage two pairs of hands dragged him away from their leader. Dan struggled to break loose. Butch scrambled to his feet, his eyes alight with fire and hate. Eager for revenge he moved forward snarling like a great bear. As he twisted to free himself from the strong grip Dan measured the distance carefully then with a vicious kick into the pit of Butch's stomach sent him writhing in pain across the ground.

From that moment Dan didn't know how

many or how often the blows hit him. He tried to defend himself and fight back but it was no use. Blow after blow pounded his face, heavy boots dug into his ribs and thighs every time he hit the ground. Through it all he was aware of the heavy breathing and panting of the four men who went about the job with a thoroughness which showed that this was not the first time they had performed such a task.

Dan struck the ground beneath a tree dully aware of the pain; blood flowed from his nose and his left eye felt as if it had been kicked by a mule. He struggled to twist out of the way expecting his attackers to deliver a few blows with their feet before picking him up. But none came. Instead a soft but firm voice drifted to his ears.

'Thet will do!'

Butch had called his sidekicks off! Dan's thoughts whirled. That wasn't Butch's voice! Then Dan was aware that two cowboys knelt beside him.

'It's all right, Dan. Take it easy. I reckon you'd hev had a lot more if we hadn't come along.'

Slowly his vision cleared and his eyes focused on the two men beside him. Suddenly he started. They were masked! A cold wet neckerchief brought relief as it was laid on his forehead by a third masked man. Dan struggled into a sitting position to see Butch and his cronies standing mute in front of two Colts in the hands of a fourth cowboy whose identity was cloaked in a neckerchief across the lower half of his face. Their guns lay in a heap a few yards away and they glared at the newcomers like cornered animals.

Dan was helped to his feet. He felt his bruised limbs and winced with the soreness as he moved.

The man who held the guns spoke. 'Take it easy, Dan, we'll deal with these rough-necks. I reckon a five mile walk back to town in this sun will do them good.'

Butch started to protest only to be silenced by a blow in the mouth from one of the other masked cowboys who snapped, 'No one's askin' you.' He walked across to the horses standing on the trail. Swiftly he stripped the saddles from four of them and sent the horses galloping away in the opposite direc-tion to Red Springs. The leader of the masked riders motioned with his guns and the Circle C boys shuffled to the trail.

'Pick up your saddles,' he snapped, 'an' enjoy your walk to Red Springs.'

With muttered oaths they reluctantly collected their gear as two masked cowboys swung on to their horses. Slowly the comic procession headed for town. Butch and his sidekicks stumbled as they struggled with their saddles along the hard trail under the hot sun. The two riders laughed as they goaded the roughnecks on and in spite of his sore face Dan grinned at the sight.

As they disappeared round the bend in the road Dan turned to the two remaining rescuers.

'I shore want to thank you fer your help.'

'Sorry we weren't sooner, son,' apologised the shorter of the two removing his mask.

'Clint!' Dan shouted leaping forward and slapping the older man on the back. 'But who's this?' he asked indicating the other man.

Slowly the leader removed his mask.

'Mr Collins!' gasped Dan. 'Why – how–?' he stammered in amazement.

Collins grinned. A fine upright man with jet black hair, he was neatly turned out in good, everyday working clothes. 'I reckon you took a beatin' Dan, but I shore think you'd hev been worse off if it hadn't been fer old Clint here.'

'I'm shore grateful to you all,' said Dan

turning to his old friend for an explanation.

'Wal, I reckoned you were in bad company when you left the saloon,' drawled Clint, 'an' I figured I'd better do somethin' about it. There weren't much I could do on my own an' I figured if you'd been home you'd seen Miss Barbara an' I reckoned she would influence her Pa into helpin' you. When I told her the story thet gal didn't waste a second. We had horses saddled like lightnin' and sought out her Pa and two brothers.'

'Thet's where the delay came in,' interrupted Mr Collins. 'We were out in Crows Valley but Barbara lost no time in tellin' us your story. Wal thet shore altered our minds about you an' if Barbara was convinced thet was good enough fer us so we hit the trail mighty quick, besides those hombres ain't to our likin'.'

'But why the masks?' asked Dan.

'Thet was Clint's idea,' answered Mr Collins.

'Shore, I figured if you an' I were goin' to track down these here rustlers then some help would be most acceptable an' we'd all be of more use if we were unknown.'

Dan grinned. He felt a new man at the news. Now he had four friends to ride by his side. He gripped their hands.

As they swung into the saddle and headed for Red Springs, Dan made a request. 'I'm shore glad to hev your help but there's one stipulation.'

'What's thet?' asked Clint.

'When it comes to the final showdown Wes Brown's my man – a three years old memory has got to be wiped out!'

Chapter 5

The three riders took a short cut across country and slipped into Red Springs by way of the side streets. They made their way unseen to the McCoy house and found an anxious, worried Barbara awaiting them. At the sound of hoofs clopping the road she hurried to the door and ran outside to meet the three men as they dismounted.

'Dan! Oh, Dan are you all right?' A worried frown puckered her brow above troubled eyes which looked anxiously at the young man as he eased his bruised body out of the saddle.

Dan smiled and nodded as Barbara gripped his arm and hurried him towards the house.

'Dad,' she called over her shoulder, 'come and help. Clint, see to the horses, please.'

'Shore, lassie,' answered the grizzled faced cowboy. 'You go on in, Mr Collins, I'll be with you in a few moments.' He gathered the reins and led the horses to the stable while Bill Collins hurried after his daughter.

Dan insisted that he felt fine but Barbara thought otherwise and soon she was bathing his bruised face. The young man winced as the hot water touched his wounds but as the gentle fingers soothingly went about their task he thought the beating was almost worth it. Barbara heard the story from her father who soon had some hot coffee ready. A thoughtful Clint joined them and the three cowboys discussed the situation whilst Barbara prepared a meal.

The clop of horses hoofs brought Bill Collins to his feet. He peered cautiously through the window.

'It's all right,' he commented with relief. 'It's only the boys.'

Their tale of the sweating, struggling Butch and his cronies amused the listeners.

'Jest what they deserved,' laughed Clint. 'They shore are a no good bunch.'

'They were about all in when we left them half a mile out of town,' grinned Jack Collins.

'Anyone see you?' asked their father.

'No one,' replied Howard Collins. 'We rode back along the trail an' circled before comin' here. No one can suspect us.'

'Good work,' laughed Clint slapping the table. 'Thet means Brown will hev four un-known riders agin him. What you figure on doin', Dan?'

'Wal, we ain't much to go on,' answered the ex-sheriff, 'so we can't force the issue. We'll hev to keep watch an' await developments. Now, we know Brown an' Fennell are cronies.' He paused and glanced at Barbara as he made this statement but she made no sign at the mention of Fennell's name. 'We can keep tail on Wes but only with difficulty an' risk of discovery but Fennell's a different kettle of fish. He's around town an' his movements are goin' to be easier to follow.'

'But Fennell's the sheriff,' cut in Jack.

Dan quirked his eyebrows. 'What odds, there's been crooked sheriffs before today.'

'There's been nothin' suspicious agin him so far,' pointed out Howard sipping his coffee.

'Agreed, everythin' appears all right on the surface but I hev a hunch thet Fennell's in on this thing; an' I believe in followin' hunches so that means followin' Fennell. From those few words I heard on the trail Brown an' Fennel are meetin' tonight an' I aim to tail the sheriff.'

Barbara spun round from the sink. 'Oh, no, you're not! It's a good night's rest for you. No creepin' about in the dark, you've had enough for one day.'

Dan's face reddened at the orders and the smiles of the four men.

'Barbara's right, Dan,' spoke up Mr Collins pulling his pipe from his pocket. 'We're all in this now. Jack an' Howard can do thet job between 'em.'

Dan started to protest but saw it was useless. 'All right,' he said. 'Keep close to him. I reckon you'll learn somethin'.'

Clint looked shrewdly at Dan. 'You figure Brown's goin' to rustle Wayman's cattle.'

'Wal, Wayman's got a mighty fine herd an' if he loses it he's goin' to be in a sorry state; remember, his ranch borders the Circle C an' he almost sold out to Hiram Griffiths when his cattle were rustled before.'

'Then you think Griffiths is behind it all?' asked Collins lighting his pipe.

'Maybe, maybe not. Brown could be playin' a deeper game.'

'Wal, if you figure correctly,' muttered Clint half to himself as if echoing deep thoughts, 'then somethin's goin' to happen mighty soon 'cause Wayman'll be movin' them cattle within the next twenty-four hours. Bill, I reckon you an' I'll go out there an' keep our eyes open.'

Mr Collins puffed at his pipe and nodded agreement.

'Dan, you stay here an' rest. Jack an' Howard keep your eyes on Fennell; Clint and I'll take up position on Smokey Rocks. We can see the whole valley from there. Barbara, pack us some more grub, please.'

Dan started to protest at being left out but accepted the situation on condition that he would be kept informed of any developments.

After giving their horses a quick rub down Jack and Howard Collins rode into town. The sun was beginning to settle in the western sky and the shadows in the small Texan town were lengthening.

They hitched their horses to the rail outside the saloon glancing through the windows as they strolled along the sidewalk. The man they were looking for was not inside so they continued their casual walk heading in the direction of the sheriff's office. Their man was not on the main street so they entered the lawman's office and were relieved to find him seated at his desk. He glanced up sharply as they entered.

'Hello, Luke,' drawled Howard seating himself on the corner of the desk while Jack dropped into a chair.

'Howdy boys,' greeted Fennell leaning back in his chair. 'What can I do fer you?'

'Nothin' fer us,' answered Howard. 'It's Barbara.'

'Anythin' wrong?' Luke was startled. 'Thet fellow McCoy been pesterin' her?' he added quickly. 'You know, I reckon you should persuade Barbara to leave thet house.'

'Wal, won't she when she marries you?' drawled Jack.

'Yeah, shore, but I–'

'Besides,' cut in Howard, 'why are you bothered about McCoy, we jest heard he'd been run out of town.'

'Shore, he was,' muttered the sheriff. 'Butch, Al an' a couple of other Circle C boys.' Anger clouded his face. 'But a gang of masked riders rescued him an' Butch an' his pardners hed to hoof it back to town.'

'What! Masked men!' The brothers appeared startled.

'Yeah. So it wouldn't surprise me if McCoy comes back. I hear Wes Brown warned him against doin' so but if he's around here again I'll see he's run out of town once fer all.'

The brothers grinned to themselves remembering their sister's description of Luke's last meeting with Dan.

'Wal, don't worry too much about him,' advised Jack with a wink at his brother as they saw the streak of jealousy in Fennell.

'I'm shore Babs hasn't any time fer him or why would she ask us to call an' tell you she'll be expectin' you to call later on?'

Relief showed in the sheriff's face. 'Wal, thet's all right. You hed me worried fer a moment, I thought somethin' was wrong, but I'm afraid you'll hev to tell Barbara thet I won't be able to make it. I've a job on.'

'Thet's too bad,' drawled Howard. 'Babs will be disappointed.' He grinned at Jack.

'Thet's one thing your sister will hev to git used to when she's married to a lawman. I can't always be around.'

'O.K. We'll tell her,' said Jack pushing himself from his chair. 'Comin' Howard?'

'Right, Jack.' Howard swung slowly round off the desk. 'See you later Luke.'

'So long, boys,' answered the sheriff.

'How right you are, Howard,' grinned Jack as they closed the office door. 'We'll shore see thet smooth customer again, mighty soon.'

The brothers strolled across the street and slumped into a couple of chairs in front of the hotel.

Light was fading from the sky when Luke Fennell, pulling on his Stetson, emerged from his office. He glanced up and down the street, waved to the two brothers who saluted him casually, and climbing into the saddle

71

turned his horse southwards out of Red Springs.

Jack and Howard Collins gazed after the figure of the sheriff without a word until he reached the outskirts of the town.

'C'm on, Jack,' snapped Howard jumping out of his chair. 'Things are startin' to move.'

They hurried along the sidewalk, testing the hang of their guns. They unhitched their horses, swung into the saddles and rode southwards at a steady lope.

As they left the town they espied the outline of a rider in the gathering dusk. Not a word was spoken. They followed at a steady pace closing the distance a little as the darkness spread across the Texas countryside endeavouring to hide the lone rider from the brothers.

The trail climbed steadily for about a mile and they nodded to each other as a silhouette appeared on the skyline and dropped out of sight over the ridge. Jack and Howard urged their horses forward to gain on the sheriff whilst out of his sight. As they neared the top of the rise they left the road and crept carefully up the hill so that they would not be silhouetted on the trail. Quickly they slid over the hill and swung back to the trail noting that their quarry was still following the hard road at a steady lope.

Half a mile further on Luke passed from sight as the road twisted between huge rocks and dropped amongst some trees towards a wide stream which rippled across a stony ford. It was dark beside the stream where the cottonwoods thickened to hide the waning light. Jack was startled. There was no sign of Luke Fennell ahead.

'Guess he must hev quickened his pace an' be round thet bend,' whispered Jack as the brothers urged their horses into the water. The animals stepped carefully across the ford as the water swished round their fetlocks and their hoofs stubbed against hidden stones.

With a relief that trembled through their bodies the horses scrambled up the bank on to dry ground and moved forward along the trail. They had gone but a few paces when Howard reined his mount to a standstill and slid quietly out of the saddle. He dropped to his knees and examined the ground carefully. Without a word he walked a few paces forward and once again crouched to scan the road. He straightened quickly and hastened to Jack who had pulled up alongside Howard's horse.

'What's wrong, Howard?' whispered Jack.

'Fennell didn't come this way. There are no fresh tracks, only ours; the ground's dry!'

'Wal, I'll be durned,' gasped Jack as he swung out of the saddle. 'You shore?'

'Certain,' answered Howard. 'Let's scout around.'

The two cowboys moved along the trail but finding no signs returned to the bank of the stream. They examined the ground carefully but failed to find any tracks of a third horse.

'Maybe he didn't cross the ford,' muttered Jack quietly.

'Fools! We took it fer granted thet he did; remember he'd be out of sight when he reached the stream.'

They hurried back to their horses, swung into their saddles and hastened their animals back across the ford. They had hardly left the water before they were once again examining the ground. Howard walked slowly back along the trail pausing now and then to examine the ground. Suddenly he grunted with satisfaction, turned on his heels and carefully followed the hoof marks he had seen. He called softly to his brother who hurried to join him and together they followed the tracks to the water's edge. They looked at each other with surprise.

'Wal, he shore entered the water but didn't come out at the other side.' Jack tugged at his right ear, a puzzled frown furrowing his forehead.

'D'ya reckon he's rumbled us?' questioned Howard a worried tone in his voice.

'Don't see how he could, we've kept well back an' he shore didn't turn round whilst we hed him in sight. No, I reckon this makes this meetin' even more suspicious. He's hidin' his trail as a precaution an' headin' fer some secret meetin' place. Reckon he went up or down stream fer some ways.'

'Guess you're right Jack. I suppose he could hev swung back on to this bank but I figure he wouldn't come to this here stream jest fer the pleasure of gettin' wet. We'll try the far bank. You work down-stream an' I'll go up. If you find anythin' give two thrush calls.'

Jack nodded and once more they crossed the ford. After tying their horses to a convenient branch they separated, each keeping close to the bank side, examining the ground carefully for any sign which would indicate that a horse had left the water.

Howard had covered about half a mile before he noticed imprints on the soft bank.

Quickly he surveyed them and decided that they matched those he had followed to the water. Facing down stream he cupped his hands round his mouth and a thrush called gaily. He tilted his head listening for the reply. When it came he followed the hoof marks through the trees until they came on to a track which climbed a small hill. Satisfied that they headed for the hill, Howard returned to the water's edge to await his brother. It was not long before he heard the sound of horses splashing through the stream. Once again he imitated the thrush and an answering call came from close at hand. Gradually from the darkness there emerged the silhouettes of two horses and one rider.

'Quick, over here,' called Howard quietly.

Soon Howard was mounted and leading his brother to the track on the hill. Before reaching the top Jack called to Howard to stop. He slipped from the saddle and crept steadily to the top of the rise. Howard saw his brother peer cautiously over the top then quickly turn and run back.

'I think we've found the place,' he panted as he joined Howard. 'There's a cabin in a little hollow over the top. C'm on, hurry, we may be too late as it is. Let's hide the horses amongst that clump of rocks. If we work over from there I reckon we should come down behind the cabin.'

With the horses secured out of sight the two brothers crept stealthily down the bank to the cabin. They paused against the back wall of the timbered hut. Voices came from inside.

'Round the front,' whispered Howard.

Cautiously the Collins boys crept round the building and flattened themselves alongside a window, a blind was drawn but chinks of light showed down the side. A couple of panes of glass were broken and the brothers could easily distinguish the voices of Brown and Fennell.

'Now, you know your part in the plan. Pull this off an' we're made,' laughed Brown. 'Wayman will hev to sell this time.'

Fennell chuckled. 'If only he knew the protection he's goin' to get. Say, Wes, if we're forcing Wayman to sell then I gather Hiram Griffiths is the boss?'

Brown smashed his fist on to the table. 'I've told you before, Fennell, don't get curious; it ain't healthy.'

'Then who was it I saw leavin' here?' snapped Luke.

Brown's chair fell with a crash as he sprang

to his feet. 'You been around here afore you should,' he snarled. 'You're startin' to over-play your hand, Luke, keep it as it is an' you'll be all right.' His voice went quiet but it carried a high powered meaning. 'Don't git curious any more or else you'll end up the same way as old man McCoy.'

'If it ain't Griffiths, then it's you Wes an' you're playin' a deeper game than I know.' His chair scraped the floor as he pushed it back and stood up. 'Remember Wes, I'm in this; be sure to give me a fair deal.'

'You can trust me but don't git too inquisitive. Now fergit it an' let's git goin', there's a lot to be done.'

The Collins brothers were about to move away, cursing their luck in losing the trail and missing plans which had been made, when they were halted by Brown's next remark.

'My men will be in a position before dawn, we'll move in at first light. Be sure you're on the opposite side of the valley; then you can prevent the herd from turning that way at the same time appearing to stop us.'

In the darkness Jack Collins nudged his brother. Quietly they moved round to the back of the hut and with guns drawn waited.

They heard the door close and the two men walk towards their horses across the hollow. Howard crept to the corner of the shack and watched the shadowy figures mount and ride away. He remained silent until he saw them break the sky-line then he motioned to his brother. They scrambled up the hill and hurried to their horses. They rode cautiously at first taking a different way to the south road from Red Springs. Once they reined their horses to a stop and spoke for the first time.

'Seems Dan's theories were right,' observed Jack.

'Yeah. An' we've got to act quickly, the show must start at dawn,' replied Howard easing himself in the saddle.

'You ride to Smokey Rocks an' join Dad an' Clint. Stay there with 'em. I'll let Dan know what's happened an' we'll join you out there. If I know Dan he'll not be left out of this show.'

'Right,' answered his brother turning his horse on the trail. 'So long.' He kicked his horse into a gallop and headed south turning toward the Brazo River.

Jack watched his brother disappear into the darkness then quirted his horse into a gallop towards Red Springs.

Chapter 6

Jack Collins covered the distance to Red Springs quickly but slowed his horse to a walk when he neared the town. He noticed a light in the sheriff's office and Luke's horse tied to the rail outside. The town was quiet, only the sound of a piano mingled with shouts and laughter from the saloon disturbed the silence of the Texas night.

Jack turned from the main street and halted his horse outside the McCoy house. He hurried up the path to find that Barbara had not gone to bed.

'Jack! You all right? Where's Howard!' she asked anxiously.

'Steady, Sis,' he smiled. 'I'm O.K. Howard's gone to Smokey Rocks. Get Dan, quick,' he urged.

'You needn't bother, Babs,' Dan's voice was quiet as he entered the room. 'I heard someone coming up the path and saw it was you.'

'Dan, you should still be in bed,' admonished Barbara.

Dan smiled, kissed her lightly on the cheek and with a disarming look in his eyes said, 'Babs, darling, Jack has somethin' urgent to tell me, I can feel it in my bones, an' I'm not goin' to be left out of it any longer.'

Barbara shrugged her shoulders realising that it was useless to keep this tough cowboy inactive any longer.

'Right, Jack, out with your story,' urged Dan as he pulled a chair from under the table and sat down. Jack threw his Stetson on to the table and sat down opposite him.

'How about some coffee?' said Jack.

Barbara smiled at the demands of men and put a kettle on the fire.

Jack related his story quickly.

'Sorry we slipped up,' he apologised when he finished his tale.

'Slipped up? You've done grand work. We know they are goin' to attempt to rustle Wayman's cattle an' what's more important we know when. The only thing we are not sure of is the direction of the attack.'

'No, but we do know that Luke will be on the opposite side of the valley to Wes.'

Dan slapped the table. 'Right,' he shouted. 'That's it, Jack, I'll join the others at Smokey Rocks, you keep trail on Fennell. As soon as you know where he's goin' to position himself let us know – thet will narrow down the area to watch.'

The two cowboys hastened their preparations and were soon ready to leave.

'I'll not waken Ma,' said Dan fastening his gun belt.

Barbara watched with a heavy heart as the tall lithe man tied his holsters to his legs. She did not speak and in that moment realised that she still loved Dan. It had only required some explanation from him to ease the doubts created three years ago. She packed them some food and with tears in her eyes watched the two men leave the house.

Jack helped Dan to saddle his horse before they left separately. Jack went no further than the main street of Red Springs where a light still shone in the sheriff's office. He stopped outside the saloon, strolled inside, bought himself a drink and sat down beside a window from which he could keep the lawman's office under observation.

Half an hour passed without any movement across the street. Suddenly the sound of horses hoofs from the south end of town sharpened his attention. Jack frowned. He hoped Dan hadn't run into them as he headed south. He tipped his glass back and hurried outside to see the riders pulling up outside the sheriff's office. He strolled casually along the sidewalk straining to identify the riders as they passed through the pool of light spilling through the doorway. Collins gasped, 'Circle C boys!'

He leaned on the rail for a few moments and as there were no further developments he strolled back to the saloon to take up his position near the window once more. A quarter of an hour went by before the sheriff's door opened. Six cowboys came out; the light in the office was put out and in the faint light cast by the stars and new moon Jack saw shadowy figures cross the street towards the saloon.

The six riders clattered through the batwings and a moment later were joined by Luke Fennell. They lined the bar and called to Blackie. The sheriff glanced round the room, picked up his drink and crossed the floor to Jack.

'Did you give Barbara my message?' he asked.

'Shore, Luke. She was mighty sorry you wouldn't be round,' he replied then nodded an invitation to sit down.

'Can't, thanks all the same. Thet job's keepin' me busy. Wayman's movin' his herd an' after what happened before he's afraid of rustlers so I'm out on a protectin' job – got some of the Circle C boys roped in this time.' He drained his glass. 'Guess we must be goin'. So long.'

'So long,' answered Jack with a nod.

'Come on, boys,' called Luke.

The Circle C bunch finished their drinks quickly and followed the sheriff across the street to their horses.

Jack watched them ride out of town before he left the saloon, mounted his horse and set off on his second job of trailing.

The lone cowboy was puzzled as he followed the seven riders. Brown had split his force of cowpunchers and would have difficulty in managing a herd of this size with the cowboys left at his disposal. This thought troubled Jack until suddenly it became clear that the job was going to be easier. Brown now had cowpokes on two sides of the herd and to all appearances his riders were helping the sheriff so they couldn't be the rustlers and he couldn't do the job with the few hands he had left. Jack had to admire the carefully laid plans.

After an hour's hard riding they began a steady climb up the hills which bordered the valley. Jack saw the seven riders silhouetted against the night sky dismount at the top of the hill. Swiftly he dropped from his horse and crept Indian fashion up the hillside to within a few yards of the group of men.

He heard Fennell's voice. 'Now you all know what to do, patrol this side of the herd until we get the signal from Wes. In the meantime I'm goin' over to report to Wayman and reassure him that he has nothin' to worry about.'

The Circle C riders laughed loud at this remark.

Jack remained still until the cowboys remounted and disappeared down the hillside. Swiftly he ran back to his horse. He leaped into the saddle and urged his horse forward keeping below the sky-line for about a mile before slipping over the hill and setting his mount for Smokey Rocks across the valley. He had all the information he wanted, now he must report to Dan.

Dan had watched Jack ride away from the house before he left Red Springs by the back streets. Once on the south trail he shoved his horse into a gallop. He was glad to be on the move again after being confined to the house whilst the others were active. Now things were starting to move he could not reach his friends at Smokey Rocks too soon. The night was calm and Dan made good progress.

He was perfectly relaxed in the saddle but as the trail narrowed and twisted amongst some rocks a noise some distance ahead made him pull to a halt. He paused a moment to listen, then wheeled his horse off the trail and hid behind a huge rock. Dan peered cautiously through the darkness, a calming hand on his horse. Six riders, laughing and talking, rode by at a steady trot towards Red Springs.

Dan waited until the sound of hoofs faded in the distance, thanking his luck that he had met the riders at this point; anywhere else there was little cover and he would have been seen.

After riding a further mile Dan turned along the trail leading to John Wayman's ranch. He rode under the high bluff from which he had observed Luke Fennell leave the ranch that same morning. It seemed years ago to Dan and automatically he urged his horse forward as if trying to catch up on time. He passed the ranch and turned along the old trail close to the Brazo River. When he reached the point from which he had surveyed Wayman's herd he turned along the hillside.

A further half hour's riding brought him to a flat stretch of ground at the opposite end of which the hill was broken by a jumble of rocks which drew weird shapes against the night sky. He rode cautiously and once amongst them dismounted. He guessed his friends would be in an advantageous position overlooking the valley so leading his horse he carefully picked his way towards the edge of the hill.

'All right, cowpoke, jest raise your hands.' The cool calm voice drifted from the shadows of a nearby rock. 'No, don't try anythin',' the voice continued. 'You're covered by four Colts.' A masked figure stepped into view.

Dan was relieved. 'It's Dan here,' he called softly.

'Dan! Come over here,' the masked man called. 'We were jest bein' cautious.'

'Good,' approved Dan as Howard led him to join Mr Collins and Clint.

Dan could add little to the story which Howard had told about the tracking of Luke Fennell except to tell them that they awaited news from Jack. The four cowboys settled down keeping watch in turn and enjoying a meal from the food which Barbara had prepared.

Suddenly they were aroused from their drowsing by the sound of an approaching horse. They crouched in the shadows, guns drawn as the rider drew nearer.

'It's all right boys, it's Jack,' whispered Bill Collins. 'Reckon I'd recognise the way he sits a horse anywhere.'

Jack was soon amongst them explaining the results of his shadowing of Luke Fennell and the Circle C bunch.

'Smart work by Wes,' muttered Dan. 'Rustlin' the cattle whilst it appears his boys are protectin' it.'

'What we goin' to do, Dan,' asked Howard.

'Not quite shore yet; this takes some figurin'. If we split we'll be hopelessly out-numbered by both bunches.'

'If only we knew exactly where Wes is we might prevent thet signal bein' given,' said Jack.

'Might be anywhere on this side of the valley. It would only be a stroke of luck if we found him. Time's too short fer a systematic search.'

'Maybe it's worth it,' said Howard. 'Don't see what else we can do.'

'Dan, why not ride into Wayman's camp down yonder,' suggested Clint nodding towards the fires flickering below them in the distance. 'Tell him the whole story.'

'Nice thought, Clint, but he'd never believe me. He ordered me off his ranch; blames me fer not givin' protection when he lost his cattle afore an' he's still bitter about it, even suggested I could hev rustled 'em.'

'One of us could go,' spoke up Bill Collins.

'Don't think thet would be any good either,' said Dan. 'It would only be your word against the sheriff's an' Wayman has no cause fer suspectin' the lawman, besides with the Circle C bunch split it will appear to Wayman thet there's no threat from thet quarter. No one could persuade him we were right.'

'Guess you're right,' agreed Mr Collins filling his pipe.

'What are we goin' to do Dan?' asked Howard.

Dan looked thoughtful for a moment before he spoke.

'Clint, which way do you reckon Wayman'll take his herd?'

'I guess he'd move 'em down the valley then cut out through Longhorn Gulch.'

'An' the rustlers if they succeeded?'

'I allus reckoned thet the cattle rustled around here were driven south an' eventually found their way over the border.'

'The position of Brown's men seems to indicate a drive thet way,' said Mr Collins.

'Right,' replied Dan. 'Supposin' we stampede the herd up the valley.'

There was a moment's silence as each man pondered the idea.

'Believe you've got it son,' grinned Clint.

'It would hev to be at the right moment,' pointed out Howard.

'A good idea,' said Jack.

'We'd hev to drive 'em up the valley otherwise we'd be sendin' 'em the way the rustlers would want,' observed Bill Collins.

'Up the valley is just what we want,' agreed Dan. 'We'd be sendin' them past the camp an' they'd be prevented from spreadin' by the head of the valley an' be easier fer Wayman's bunch to control but we would hev stopped Brown an' his gang.'

'Yes, but probably only fer the time bein'. He's goin' to do all he can to git this lot an' break old man Wayman,' observed Jack.

'Shore,' agreed Dan, 'but it's goin' to give us longer to act. He'll not be able to make another attempt straight away; Wayman will be alerted thinkin' we've tried to rustle the cattle.'

'Right,' said Clint, 'it's agreed, we stampede the cattle but what about timin'.'

'We've got to do it jest before Brown makes his attempt. We'll move close to the herd an' git into action as soon as we see thet signal. When it's given there won't be a moment to lose. Once we've got the cattle movin' it's every man fer himself. Outflank the herd, keepin' 'em runnin' an' ride straight over the head of the valley. We'll meet again at Ma's.'

All muttered their agreement.

Swiftly the five cowboys slipped quietly away from Smokey Rocks and crept cautiously to the valley below. The moaning of the restless cattle drifted across the grassland and not wishing to disturb them prematurely, Dan and his companions kept about a quarter of a mile away from the herd positioning themselves half way across the valley.

As the night wore on Dan looked more and more towards the eastern horizon. At the first streak of light showing over the hills he roused his companions to a sharper watch; their eyes ever on the move watching for any unusual movement or sign which could be taken as a signal.

Above the moan of the cattle a coyote wailed three times. Dan saw Jack stiffen in the saddle.

'Thet's a poor imitation of a coyote,' he whispered.

'Sounded like the real thing to me,' commented his father.

'Jack's right,' answered Howard. 'Thet weren't a real coyote.'

'Thet's good enough fer me. Right boys,' shouted Dan, 'let's go!' He kicked his horse with his heels. The animal snorted, leaped forward and stretched itself into a full gallop. The four masked riders did likewise and spread themselves out fan-shaped riding at the herd ahead.

They yelled and shouted at the top of their voices. As they bore down on the herd they drew their Colts firing across the heads of the steers. The low moan began to rise and soon changed to a loud frightened bellow. Steers pushed against each other trying to get out of the way of the hard-riding humans who frightened them with their yelling and shouting. Cattle turned buffeting each other, horns digging into flesh. Like a wind through grass the pandemonium moved until several large steers on the far side of the herd turned to get away from the pressure forced upon them. They turned and ran bellowing, snorting and tossing their heads in panic. Once the move had been made and the lead given the whole herd broke into a mad run, hoofs pounding the earth in their wild dash to escape from the frightening upheaval behind them.

As Dan moved towards the corner of the herd he saw the shadowy figure of a cowboy wheeling his horse not knowing which way to move so swiftly had the quiet moaning changed to pandemonium. Dan flattened himself on his horse and headed straight for the other rider. As he drew near he steadied himself in the saddle and with one swift movement crashed his Colt against the cowboy as he hurled past. The rider toppled from the saddle and lay still.

Once the cattle were on the move Jack and Clint, sweat pouring from them, wheeled their horses towards the flank where they caught up to Dan.

'Mighty fine stampede,' yelled Dan with a grin as he hurtled along beside young Collins.

'Circle C!' shouted Jack.

Dan glanced over his shoulder to see a band of horsemen dropping swiftly from the hill. Bullets whistled towards them but only helped to urge the cattle faster. The three riders flattened themselves along their horses and swung alongside the herd. Clint, heels drumming his horse's flanks moved in front of his two companions.

Almost before they realised it they were on top of Wayman's camp. Cowboys were running everywhere; some already mounted rode hard trying to head the herd off. Others turned as the three riders, with the Circle C gang in pursuit, rode down upon them. Gun flashes split the dawn. Clint followed by Dan and Jack were through the camp, over the fires, past the chuck-waggon and on along the valley. Dan yelled when he saw Clint reel in the saddle.

'He's hit!' he shouted. He did not know if Jack heard him but he saw him move alongside the older man. Dan wheeled his horse on the opposite side and between them they supported the wounded man as they hurled along beside the frightened cattle.

Several of Wayman's cowboys who were already in the saddle when the stampede had started sized up the situation quickly and had reached the head of the valley where they prepared to halt the cattle on the steep slopes. The steers pounding towards them suddenly found themselves pressed tighter together in a smaller space and faced by steep banks and yelling, shooting cowboys. Bellowing longhorns faltered in their dash, twisted and turned to get away from the new menace ahead. They crashed into each other; heavy bodies acted like a wall; cattle screamed as horns ripped their flesh or fell and were trampled on as cattle wheeled in one upheaving mass.

Dan saw the halt come as if some huge solid wall had been thrown across the valley. He saw cattle twist and falter across his path; another moment and the three riders would be caught among them. Powerfully he pulled at the reins turning his horse from the frightened herd; his arms strained as he heaved his mount away pulling Clint's horse with him, pushed on the other side by Jack who had also seen the peril of being crushed by the heavy steers.

The three men set their horses straight at the steep scrub-covered hillside. Bullets from their pursuers whistled close to them. Cattle pounded a few yards up the hillside then swerved back to the grassy valley straight towards the galloping horses. Dan shouted the horses to greater efforts and felt the swish of the cattle as they swept behind them.

In the midst of the chase Wes Brown and his Circle C cowboys suddenly found themselves in the path of bellowing steers. The bunch of cowboys pulled their horses to a sliding dust-whirling stop, wheeled them round and ran before the pounding hoofs gradually up the hillside. Once above the line of cattle Wes Brown called a halt and turned his gang diagonally across the scrub climbing in the direction of the three figures who moved over the hill-top.

'It's McCoy!' called Brown. 'Five hundred dollars if anyone can get him.'

As they reached the top of the hill Dan glanced back. In all the excitement he had not realised that daylight now flooded the valley. In one quick look he saw the herd being brought under control, but frowned when he noticed the riders mounting the hillside towards them.

'You O.K. now, Clint?' he called to the older man as they set their horses towards the Brazo River.

Clint nodded gritting his teeth. 'It's in my shoulder but I'll be all right.'

Jack still rode close to the ex-deputy ready to lend a hand if necessary. All three were covered in dust and their faces marked by trickles of sweat. They eased their horses into a long steady stride and the animals relieved at the slackening of pent-up exertion covered the ground quickly and easily. Dan knew at this pace some energy would be conserved by the sweating animals and he felt that they might be glad of this before the chase was finished. He also hoped that when Brown saw their easing of speed he would be tempted to exert greater efforts to close the gap and so tire his horses sooner. The three friends glanced back frequently.

'Here they come!' yelled Jack.

Dan saw several riders spilling over the hill led by a cowboy dressed completely in black. He grinned to himself when he saw that they were quirting their horses to greater speed. Reaching the river, Dan turned along the trail in the direction of the Wayman ranch but did not increase his speed.

Jack glanced anxiously at Dan when he saw their pursuers were gaining on them. He began to urge his horse faster but Dan halted him.

'Hold this speed, we'll need some energy to cross the river,' he called.

'Cross the river!' shouted Jack in surprise.

Dan nodded. 'It's shallower behind the ranch and we should be able to swim across. If Brown keeps this pace up his horses won't have the energy to make the crossing.'

Jack grinned and admired the cool thinking cowboy by his side. He flattened himself on his horse and wondered how his father and Howard were faring. The crash of gunfire called his mind back to their own situation but he realised that the shooting was wild. Reaching the point where the trail swung round the Wayman ranch Dan, followed by Clint and Jack crashed through the trees and raced towards the river.

'Straight in,' he called. 'See Clint across, Jack, an' take my horse. I'll hold 'em off for a while.'

Jack started to protest but Dan silenced him. He leaped from his horse throwing the reins to Jack. The two cowboys urged their three horses into the water and soon the cold river was up to their withers and the swim for the opposite bank had begun.

Dan ran a few yards along the river bank before dropping behind a tree. Hoofs pounded the trail. A shout indicated that the cowboys in the water had been seen and Brown urged his men towards the river bank. Dan waited a moment then fired with telling effect at the approaching gang. Taken completely by surprise they leaped from their horses with a yell and dived for cover. Shots echoed through the trees but Dan kept moving along the river bank drawing the attention of the pursuers away from the men in the water. He saw that his friends were making steady progress and provided Brown didn't get wise to his tactics he would soon be able to slip away.

He kept up a steady fire, moving his position whenever the opportunity arose. Lead poured from Circle C guns but suddenly all went quiet. Dan peered cautiously through the trees suspicious that new tactics were being employed. A rustling amongst the bushes to his left caused Dan to turn. At the same moment Colts spat death towards him. He hurled himself to one side firing at the bushes. He heard a scream and a cowboy pitched forward to lay still. At the same moment shots came from amongst the trees. Dan poured a volley of lead in that direction then moved swiftly along the river bank.

Seeing that Jack and Clint were over half way across the river he slipped close to the water's edge. He paused to empty his guns in the direction of his attackers then swiftly slid into the cold swirling water beneath the shelter of some trees.

He struck out rapidly from the bank and had gained several yards before a shout told him that his escape had been discovered. Taking a deep breath he plunged beneath the surface letting the river carry him downstream. When he broke water he saw Brown and his Circle C bunch lining the bank.

'There he is,' yelled Brown.

Shots poured in Dan's direction as he sank beneath the water once again. Frustrated cowboys ran along the river bank but when Dan came to the surface he had been carried out of range. He struck out for the opposite bank and noticed that Jack was riding rapidly to meet him.

After the strain of the stampede and exhausting ride the swim began to tell on Dan and as the current became stronger he felt his energy being sapped. He was swirled and tossed by the water. His arms ached from the fight with the swirling river. Suddenly he became aware of the dull roar and realised he was being swept towards Dullknife Cauldron, a point at which the river plunged between rocky walls and boiled over huge boulders.

Dan struck out harder mustering all his remaining energy to fight the tugging waters. They had carried him away from the bullets but now endeavoured to plunge him to his death. His muscles strained, his brain pounded as he made some headway against his would-be killer. He exerted every ounce of effort in his bid to escape. Gasping and straining he gained a few feet and was aware that Jack was yelling from the bank. Through spray-splashed eyes he saw him whirl his lariat above his head. The rope flew through the air and snaked across the water in front of Dan. He grabbed at it as the waters whisked it away but his fingers closed round the life-saving lariat.

'Hang on,' yelled Jack. Quickly he twisted the rope round the saddle horn and kicked his heels into his horse. The animal moved forward straining against the pull of the water on the cowboy. The rope went taut; the horse faltered; Jack shouted to the animal fighting against the pull of the saddle and then steadily it moved forward. It seemed like eternity to Dan before the bank began to get nearer. Slowly the horse dragged him forward. Jack slipped from the saddle still urging the sweating animal onward. He ran to the bank, plunged waist deep into the water, grasped Dan under the arms and dragged him to the bank.

Both men flopped to the ground gasping for breath. They lay for a few minutes, Dan loving the air which flowed into his aching lungs. Jack got to his feet, called to his horse which trotted back to him. He recoiled his lariat, swung into the saddle and soon returned with Dan's horse. Dan panted his thanks, climbed on to the horse and they hastened to join Clint. They found him nursing his wound watching the river from the cover of some bushes.

'Fired a few warnin' shots in case them coyotes thought of crossin' the river but I reckon their horses were too exhausted after the chase,' he said. 'You shore hed me scared fer a while Dan.'

'Wal, I reckon we've had a right successful morning,' said Dan. 'Come on Clint we'd better git you some attention fer that shoulder.' The three friends climbed into their saddles and followed the river to the next ford where they crossed and swung across country to approach Red Springs unnoticed from the north-west.

Jack hurried for the doctor who soon had Clint's shoulder patched up and reported that there was little to worry about. Unknown to the doctor, however, Dan and his friends were perturbed about the fate of Howard and his father. Their fears were short lived when the clop of horses hoofs heralded the return of Bill Collins and his son.

'We had little trouble,' related Bill enjoying his pipe after having Dan's story over a meal. 'Once the herd was under way I swung to join Howard. The steers served us well for they scattered Fennell's party. Some made for the head of the valley to help turn the cattle whilst others had all their work cut out keepin' out of the way of them tramplin' hoofs. We realised our best way of escape was over the hill to the right. I think everyone was too preoccupied with you an' the herd to notice us so we laid low at the top an' watched proceedings. Wayman's boys together with Fennell's party checked the herd an' kept it millin' round until it tired itself. I guess Wayman won't move fer a day or two.'

'Good,' answered Dan. 'We've delayed things fer the time being. Brown will strike again an' we've got to git wind of his intentions.'

Had Dan known it, events were taking place in the Wayman camp which were going to save him the trouble.

Chapter 7

John Wayman was shaken by the unexpected sound of the shots on the range
and as his precious cattle started their run
he sized up the situation quickly, leaped on
to his horse yelling for the men in camp to
follow him. The bellowing cattle were upon
them, racing past the camp and along the
valley. Wayman saw that the best chance of
stopping the mad rush was at the head of
the valley. He lashed his horse into a gallop
and the powerful, broad-chested animal
responded as if sensing the urgency of the
situation.

The cattle were in full run and with several
cowhands close on his heels Wayman set his
horse to outrun the herd. He flattened himself along the horse's back and with loud,
encouraging shouts urged it onward. Faster
and faster the animal flew along the grassy
valley gaining on the leading cattle with each
step. It seemed a life-time to John Wayman
before he was level with the leaders. A swift
glance over his shoulder reassured him that

his men were close behind.

He dug his heels into the animal. It lengthened its stride, slowly pulling ahead of the leading steers. The head of the valley rushed towards them. Suddenly they hit the hillside. The horse crashed through the scrub and carefully calculating the distance Wayman pulled his mount to a dust whirling standstill. He wheeled sharply to see a heaving tide of cattle-flesh hurtling towards him. His Colt in his left hand sent bullets crashing across the top of the herd. Horses slid around him and he yelled to his men to spread out. He had no time to acknowledge them but he was relieved to see Fennell and some of the Circle C outfit galloping to his help. Colts crashed; cowboys yelled. Wayman thought the leading steers were never going to give way when suddenly the stream parted, swirled and turned upon itself.

He breathed more freely as he saw the heaving mass slowly come under control of the cowboys who rode in upon it. It was only then that he realised that three cowboys close to the hilltop were being pursued by another bunch of riders.

Wayman was puzzled. He wiped his face with his handkerchief, eased himself in the saddle and turned his attention back to the herd. His cowboys aided by those from the Circle C had the situation well in hand and were beginning to drive the herd gently back towards the camp.

'Thet shore was some run,' said Luke Fennell. He wiped the back of his hand across his parched lips and pushed his Stetson off his forehead.

'Shore was an' I'm mighty grateful you an' the Circle C bunch were around.'

'Seems your fear of rustlers was right, John.'

Wayman grunted. 'Can't make it out. Whose thet bunch ridin' hell fer leather up thet hillside?'

Luke smiled. 'Thet's Wes Brown an' the rest of Circle C.'

'Brown?' Wayman gasped in astonishment eyeing the sheriff with some doubt.

'Shore. You see I figured this herd was a pretty big one to watch so I persuaded Wes to patrol the opposite side of the valley to me. Guess it's jest as well. Seems he had the luck an' jumped the rustlers jest as they were startin' in on the herd.'

'Wal I'll be durned. I didn't figure he was around.'

'I don't figure the rustlers' idea is drivin' this way,' said Fennell biting his lips. 'Surely

106

they didn't intend takin' the cattle straight over the top.'

'Wal it don't matter now we've stopped them,' answered Wayman. 'C'm on let's git back to camp.'

They walked their horses slowly and after making sure that the herd had settled down rode into camp to await the return of Wes Brown.

Almost an hour went by before Brown and his riders were sighted. Wayman hurried forward.

'Fine work Wes,' he called. 'Shore mighty glad you were around.'

As Brown slipped from the saddle Fennell shot him a warning glance. 'I've explained to John how we played a hunch an' hed you patrol this side of the valley.'

'Shore,' smiled Brown. 'Only too glad to help.'

'Wal, who was it, Wes?' asked Wayman eagerly.

The cowboy took the coffee which was offered to him and sipped before he spoke.

'Dan McCoy!' he announced dramatically.

'McCoy!' Wayman jumped as if he had been stung. 'The yaller-bellied coyote. I knew it; said as much to him yesterday; thet

107

he could hev rustled my cattle three years ago.'

'Wal, here's proof now, John. He's tried it again,' pointed out Fennell.

'Shore; but who was with him?'

'Dunno,' drawled Wes. 'His sidekicks were masked.'

'I figure he's brought a gang back with him from up north,' commented Fennell.

'But how'd he know I'd built up my herd agin?' puzzled the rancher frowning heavily.

'Reckon he could hev got word from here. He hed friends you know,' pointed out Brown.

'Guess you're figurin' along the right lines,' agreed Wayman. 'Did you git the skunk?'

Brown sipped at his coffee. 'Nope. He got away across the Brazo. We winged one but he got Shorty.'

'Too bad,' sympathised the rancher. 'Git yourself some grub an' then we'll head fer town.'

'Town?' asked Wes.

'Shore, I'm goin' to take some of the boys in an' see if we can git a lead on McCoy. I'd be mighty grateful if you'd come along with some of the Circle C.'

'Shore, shore,' muttered Wes. 'But what about the herd?'

'I'm not movin' it whilst this gang's about. Git some grub an' we'll ride.' Wayman moved towards the chuck wagon. Suddenly he stopped as he passed a young cowboy. 'Ain't you McCoy's brother?' he asked coldly.

Frank nodded.

The cattleman glared angrily. 'Then git out of here,' he yelled.

Brown laid a restraining hand on Wayman's arm. 'Steady, John, he rides fer me.'

'How do you know he ain't been tippin' his brother off?' snarled the rancher.

'I know he hasn't,' answered Wes firmly. 'I can vouch fer him.'

Wayman hesitated. 'All right,' he said slowly. 'I'm sorry. I guess seein' a McCoy riled me.'

When they had collected their grub from the chuck wagon Brown and Fennell wandered away from the other cowboys.

'McCoy shore upset things but he's played into our hands,' grinned Brown.

'How you mean?' asked Fennell.

'Numb head, don't you see? String along with Wayman an' git rid of McCoy an' Wayman'll shore trust us. Then when he moves his herd he won't be prepared fer rustlers; we can jump it on the way.'

'Shore thet's fine,' grinned Luke, 'but first we got to find McCoy.'

'Wal ain't we got Frank,' laughed Wes.

The meal over, Wayman with six of his cowboys accompanied by the sheriff, Brown and the Circle C riders headed for Red Springs.

'If you winged one of them, Wes, I guess he'd need a doctor,' said Wayman. 'Reckon we'll check there first.'

Wes nodded his agreement but they found the doctor was not at home.

'Come over fer a drink,' said Brown as they left the doctor's house.

'We ain't no time fer drinkin', Brown,' muttered Wayman angrily.

'I've an idea, Wayman, an' I figure we cin talk whilst the boys down a glass or two; I reckon they've earned it.'

Wayman grunted and followed Brown and Fennell to the saloon.

Seated in one corner Wes outlined his plan.

'Frank McCoy shore hates his brother an' I figure McCoy will hev been around his Ma; now maybe she knows where he is an' if she doesn't I guess Dan will pay her a visit before long her being ill. Now I figure Frank could maybe learn something if he pays her a call.'

'Right,' Wayman agreed. 'Try anythin' to git the durned coyote.'

Wes called Frank over and quickly gave him his orders.

Frank made no comment. He drained his glass and with a nod to the three men left the saloon. He hurried to his mother's house but paused when he reached the gate. He looked around, no one was in sight. He hitched up his belt and felt reassured in the touch of his guns. He pushed open the gate and walked slowly up the path. Opening the door he stepped inside. His hand flew to his gun and before anyone in the room realised what was happening they were staring into the cold muzzle of a Colt.

'Frank!' gasped Dan staring at his white-faced young brother who glanced nervously round the room. 'What you want?' Dan continued calmly.

Frank did not answer.

'Put that gun away,' advised Mr Collins. 'Things are likely to happen.'

'You said it, Mr Collins,' snapped the young man. 'Things shore are likely to happen. Don't you know thet as well as a yalla-bellied coward you've got a rustler here?'

'Rustler?'

'Yeah, my brother Dan,' snarled Frank. 'Tried to rustle Mr Wayman's herd this morning, only Wes Brown an' Luke Fennell were too smart fer him.'

Mr Collins whistled. 'Wayman's herd! Thet shore would hev been some haul. But how d'ya know it was Dan? Besides how could he do it on his own?'

'Saw him myself; helped chase him, an' he wasn't on his own. He hed two masked riders with him an' there are others about. Reckon he brought 'em from up north. Wayman wants you, Dan, an' I'm takin' you in. Git movin'!' Frank motioned with his gun.

'Don't be a fool,' snapped Dan.

'You'd better walk.' Frank spoke from tight lips. His face was pale and drawn. 'Don't let me hev to kill you, 'cause I shore will after all the trouble you caused Ma. An' don't anyone else try any tricks,' he warned, glancing at the other occupants of the room. His eyes rested on Clint. He stared at the bandage round the older man's shoulder. 'Clint, you hurt?' he continued in a whisper.

Clint nodded.

Frank's eyes narrowed.

Dan moved as if to step forward. Frank straightened menacing with his gun.

'Don't move,' he advised strongly. 'Let's figure this out. We winged one of the masked men. Clint, your shoulder– Four of you.' He stared incredulously at the five men. 'Why, you no good coyotes,' he shouted, 'it's you, you're the masked men. Helpin' a no good coward like this; wait until my lot git to hear about this. Now come on Dan, march an' don't anyone do anythin' or else Dan gits the lot.'

Dan hesitated.

'Come on, move!' yelled Frank.

'If I was you I'd drop thet gun,' advised a quiet voice from the foot of the stairs.

Everyone was taken by surprise. No one had heard a sound.

'Mrs McCoy!' Barbara was startled as she spun round. 'You shouldn't–'

'Keep still, Barbara,' snapped Mrs McCoy as the girl moved instinctively towards her. 'Don't spoil this. I couldn't stop in bed an' let Frank make a fool of himself. You'd better drop it, Frank, this is your Pa's old Colt an' I learned to use it in the old days, there was need then. Seems there's still a need with fools like you around.'

Frank stared at his mother. Slowly his arm dropped and the gun clattered to the floor.

Mrs McCoy lowered her own gun. 'Thet's

better,' she said. 'Now try an' talk some sense into him Dan.' She turned and walked back upstairs.

For a moment no one moved then Howard picked up Frank's gun quickly and Barbara ran after the sick woman.

'Sit down, Frank,' said Dan quietly.

Frank glanced at the five men who watched his reaction carefully. He stumbled to a chair; his face drawn and white. Dan took the Colt from Howard and slipped it back into Frank's holster. The younger McCoy stared at his brother. Dan smiled.

'We know you won't draw,' he said.

'Can't very well when I'm outnumbered,' answered Frank weakly.

'Apart from thet, kid, you'll realise how wrong you are when you hear my story. I'm no coward an' I'm no rustler. When I came back here I came 'cause Ma hed sent fer me. She told me you were ridin' fer Wes Brown an' figured you'd run into trouble. She wanted me to do somethin' about it. Apart from thet I jest had to come back some day to make amends fer walkin' out three years ago.'

'I want no stories,' snapped Frank, holding his head in his hands.

'Since I returned these four old friends

114

have believed me why not–'

'You forget me.' Barbara spoke quietly as she entered the room. She walked across the room to Dan took hold of his arm and rested the other hand on Frank's shoulder. 'Frank,' she went on, 'my world crashed when Dan walked away from Wes Brown three years ago. Nobody felt it more than I did. For nights I was tormented by the sight of Dan walking out of this town but now I believe his story. I trust him; I love him; listen to him Frank and believe him.'

Frank lifted his head and stared at the girl who smiled at him with a confident sparkling light in her eyes.

'But – but–' stammered the young cowboy, 'I don't understand. What about Luke?'

'I know now that I never loved Luke; Dan has occupied my heart all the time but I guess under the circumstances it was jest natural for a girl to turn somewhere else.' Barbara turned to Dan. 'Now Dan, tell him everything.'

No one spoke as Dan told his story.

'So you see,' he finished, 'we were really preventin' Brown from rustlin' thet herd.'

'But it looked as though you were tryin' to rustle it,' pointed out Frank.

'I know an' now Brown an' Fennell hev

made it appear to Wayman thet thet is what we were doin'. Thet puts 'em in good with Wayman. Get us out of the way an' when Wayman moves thet herd he won't be on the look out fer rustlers. Ideal set up fer Brown.' Dan paused. He looked hard at his brother. 'Well there it is, Frank. You walked right in on us. Thet's the story an' now you are free to go or stay as you please. Go, an' I can't be responsible fer the consequences; stay an' you can help us.'

Frank stared at the faces around him. Clint's lips were tightened by the pain from his shoulder but his deep dark eyes showed a firmness in their belief; Jack and Howard leaned against the wall their eyes showing a trust in the cause they followed; Mr Collins watched him through the smoke which curled from his pipe with eyes which showed he believed in Dan. Frank looked at his brother and saw a resolution to see the job through and a hope that his young brother would follow him.

'All right,' he whispered. 'I'm with you.' He held out his hand and Dan clasped it firmly. 'I'm shore sorry,' Frank murmured, 'thet I misjudged you.'

The tension in the room broke and everyone started to speak at once.

116

'All right everyone, listen.' Dan shouted to make himself heard. 'Brown wants us out of the way, well we'll let him do jest thet.'

Everyone stared at Dan in amazement.

'You mean you're goin' to let 'em take us?' asked Jack incredulously.

Dan smiled. 'Jest thet or at least me. Now listen carefully.'

Around the table plans were laid which heralded the downfall of Wes Brown and Luke Fennell.

Chapter 8

The saloon in Red Springs was crowded. News of the attempted rustling had spread rapidly and the cowboys were eager for the details and ready to help track down the rustlers.

Wayman looked out of the window for the tenth time. 'What's keepin' him,' he said impatiently. 'You shore he'll play his part?'

'Certain. I've had young McCoy under my wing ever since Dan left an' after my work he shore hates his brother. You should hev seen Frank when he met him in here,' answered Brown.

'Wal, where is he? It doesn't take this long to—'

'Take it easy Mr Wayman,' cut in Wes. 'I know you want to git McCoy but maybe Frank's Ma is a bit stubborn—'

'Shore was.' A quiet drawl startled them.

Dan had stepped through the batwings so stealthily that no-one had noticed him. Silence hit the saloon; everyone stared in amazement.

'Why, you low down scum,' shouted Wayman his hand flashing towards his gun but Dan drew lightning fast.

'I wouldn't court disaster Mr Wayman, so jest keep your hands off your guns,' snapped Dan. 'And thet goes fer anyone else here.'

The tall rancher stared at the muzzle and let his gun slip back into its holster. Fennell looked anxiously at Brown who swung on the back legs of his chair looking unperturbed.

'You shore hev a nerve,' spluttered Wayman, 'comin' in here after tryin' to rustle my cattle.'

'I ain't come to talk about thet, Wayman. Some day you'll realise how wrong you are.' Dan turned his attention to the Circle C foreman. 'It's Brown I came to see.'

Brown showed no surprise but continued to swing on his chair. 'Wal?' he drawled.

'I don't like you sendin' Frank to do your dirty work. He was surprised to find me at home but he got the drop on me an' would hev hed me here if it hadn't been for Ma; she was handy with a gun in the old days.'

The three cowboys looked at Dan with surprise.

'Your Ma will hev to answer fer this,' snapped Fennell. 'Aidin' a criminal is an

119

offence agin the law.'

'You'd better not interfere with Ma,' said Dan grimly. 'An' Brown your bad influence on Frank is finished; he won't be back.'

Wes smiled but said nothing.

'You don't expect to git away with this, McCoy,' said Wayman.

'Who's goin' to stop me?' answered Dan.

'I am!' came the reply from over Dan's shoulder.

He felt hard steel pressed into his back and saw smiles break the faces in front of him.

'Nice work, Bill,' laughed Wayman. 'You shore came in at the right moment. You want to train your ears a bit more, McCoy.'

'Heard the story when I hit town jest now. Came straight over to see if there was anythin' I could do. Your man now, sheriff.'

Dan turned to see his captor. 'Bill Collins!' he gasped. 'I—'

'I'm as surprised as you, Dan. Never thought you'd return as a rustler.'

Dan did not answer but moved forward towards the door as Fennell prodded him with his gun.

'Hold it,' rapped Brown. He walked up to Dan. His face hardened. 'We want to know where your gang is, McCoy,' he hissed.

'You'd better talk or you'll git the treatment from Butch an' his pals right here an' now. I guess they'd welcome another go.'

'Shore would, boss,' grinned Butch stepping forward rubbing his hands with obvious pleasure.

'Gang?' asked Collins.

'Yeah,' replied Wayman. 'McCoy's been operatin' with masked riders; guess he brought 'em with him from up north.' Collins' jaw tightened.

'There's no need to make McCoy talk, I know where they are!'

A murmur went round the room when Collins snapped this news.

Brown looked puzzled. 'How come?' he asked.

'I've jest come in on the north road,' explained Collins. 'About five miles out I cut off across Black Ridge. I was near Cascade Hollow when I saw four masked riders.'

'That'll be them,' shouted Wayman excitedly. 'You said there were four of 'em, Wes.'

Brown nodded. 'See where they went, Collins?'

'They dismounted in the hollow an' set about gittin' some grub.'

'Guess they were waitin' there whilst McCoy came to see his Ma,' said Fennell.

'We've got McCoy here so I guess they'll still be waitin'.'

'Come on, boss, let's get after them hombres,' shouted Butch. 'I shore hev somethin' to settle with 'em.'

'Hold on, Butch. We'll do this orderly like,' cautioned Brown.

'Yeah,' agreed the sheriff. 'First things first. I'll lock this here rustler up an' then we'll ride. Move. McCoy.' Luke jabbed his gun in Dan's back and shoved him through the batwings.

Brown whispered to Butch who looked at Al and nodded to the doorway.

'Hold it, sheriff,' Butch called as he stepped on to the sidewalk.

The two cowboys crossing the dusty road stopped and turned. Luke gasped when he saw the Colt bunched in Butch's right hand. He stared incredulously at Butch and then at Wes. Dan frowned. This was something he hadn't bargained for.

'Don't worry, sheriff,' grinned Butch. 'We're takin' McCoy so jest slip thet gun back in your holster peaceable like. Gaol's too pleasant fer that coyote.' Butch shouted over his shoulder. 'I reckon we'll string him up, boys. Hangin's what a cattle thief deserves.'

Shouts of agreement came from the cowboys pressing through the batwings and spilling on to the sidewalk. Dan paled. His plan was coming unstuck. Bill Collins started forward but stopped when Dan's eyes told him to wait.

'C'm boys let's take him,' yelled Butch stepping into the thin layer of dust which covered the road.

A gun roared and Butch's Colt was blasted from his grip. He spun on his heels, grasping his wounded hand, his face screwed up with the pain. His dark eyes flashed anger at John Wayman who stood close by with smoke curling from his .45.

'Brown,' he snapped, 'keep your cowpokes in hand. I may not like McCoy but I don't approve of lynchin' either. He'll stand fair trial an' with the number of witnesses we hev I figure he'll git a sizeable term in gaol. Right, Fennell, git him under lock an' key.' The tall rancher turned to the crowd. 'We want the rest of the gang so all keep your heads. C'm on.' He slipped his gun back into its holster and moved to his horse. Fennell hurried Dan to the gaol and after putting him behind bars mounted his horse and rode to the head of the posse.

'Can't possibly get away from a bunch like

this,' laughed Fennell as horses pounded the hard trail out of Red Springs. 'Biggest posse I've ever had.'

Bill Collins who had moved up with the leaders smiled to himself as they congratulated themselves on the easy break up of the gang.

'We'll spread out an' circle the hollow an' prevent any break out,' shouted Wes to the following cowboys as they climbed towards Black Ridge. He would not have felt so confident had he known that eyes were watching their approach.

Frank McCoy, taking the place of Bill Collins as the fourth masked rider lay at the top of Cascade Hollow watching the country in the direction of Red Springs. He grinned to himself as the cloud of dust began to grow larger. He felt a sense of relief – everything seemed to be going according to plan. Turning he waved to his companions in the hollow and saw them break camp and make a hurried preparation to leave.

The cloud of dust turned towards Cascade Hollow. Frank flattened himself closer to the ground and watched the riders draw nearer. Still he did not move. Below him, Clint and the Collins boys were already mounted and watched Frank anxiously. They had to time their move so as to encourage pursuit. Still Frank waited. He saw one of the leaders raise his right arm and signal to the following horsemen. The posse split into three and as two columns started to encircle the hollow Frank slithered to his horse a short distance below him. He leaped into the saddle and saw his friends wheel their horses and urge them forward across the hollow.

'They're comin' round both sides,' yelled Frank as he drew alongside the others.

The four masked riders scrambled out of the hollow sending showers of stones and soil tumbling under the horses' hoofs. The crash of gunfire indicated that they had been seen but the range was too great to be harmful.

Riders yelled; horses thundered across Cascade Hollow, through the scrub on the rise and out on to tree-covered Black Ridge. Frank flattened himself on his horse's back as it stretched its legs in full gallop. He weaved past the trees keeping close to Clint who, in spite of his wound, had insisted on playing his part. Clint rode with a courage and a skill gained through years spent in the west. He handled his horse cleverly keeping close on the heels of the Collins boys.

Whilst maintaining a headlong gallop they

gradually moved down the ridge towards the scrub-covered plain below. The earth shook with the pounding hoofs of pursuers attempting to gain on the four riders ahead. Guns blazed but the distance was too great to be effective. Mile after mile they sped and Wayman noticing that the gap had opened a little urged the posse to greater efforts.

Across the plain the trail climbed steadily amongst craggy hills and the ground became rougher. Bill Collins had moved up with the leaders of the posse and he watched his sons and friends anxiously as the terrain grew more difficult. He was fearful lest a horse should stumble and he keyed himself ready to lend a hand should any of the four riders get into difficulties.

Suddenly Brown yelled. 'We've got 'em. They're headin' fer Death Drop Canyon.'

Bill Collins gasped. He stared incredulously watching the four riders turn along another trail hemmed in on both sides by huge walls of rock. Death Drop Canyon was a wide cleft which had cut across this old trail through the hills. Bill was worried. The four men were riding into a trap from which the only escape was to leap Death Drop Canyon. Bill's brow puckered. He had once jumped the Canyon for a bet but only a superb horseman could do it. He knew his sons had mounts capable of it and they had the courage to try. He felt sure that Frank would not hesitate to follow them over the half a mile drop but a wounded Clint was a different matter.

'They must halt,' shouted Wes triumphantly. 'They're ours.'

The horses pounded on; the walls closing in on the trail threw back the noise with a thundering echo. Jack and Howard steeled themselves as their horses flew towards the Canyon. The drop rushed at them. Horses and riders were one. They called softly to their animals whose powerful legs sent them into a great breath-taking leap across the canyon. Clint knew what lay ahead but the throb in his shoulder had begun to pain him and with the strain of holding the horse his arm had become useless. But Clint did not falter. The ex-deputy, his face strained, tensed himself. He shouted to his horse and the broad-backed animal pushed off with a power that flowed through its muscular body. Clint's superb riding carried him over safely and his horse moved straight into the same rhythmic gallop as if nothing had altered its stride.

Frank was so close to Clint that he saw the

Canyon almost too late. For a split second he checked his horse, then relaxed, gave it its head and yelled. The dark chestnut pushed off in a superb leap but the slight check had altered its stride. The animal hit the ground, its back legs on the very edge of the gap. Frank lost his balance and was flung from the horse's back to hit the trail and roll over and over in the dust, the breath driven from his body. Stones clattered from the Canyon's rim echoing to the depths below as the horse regained its foothold and scrambled away from the death drop.

Jack and Howard Collins glanced over their shoulders to see how their companions had fared. They pulled their horses to a dust raising stop and almost in the same movement wheeled them round. Howard was soon alongside Frank's chestnut calming it and steadying it along the trail. Jack yelled with all the power of his lungs. Frank stirred and scrambled to his feet when he saw Jack riding hard towards him. In a cloud of swirling dust the posse reined their horses to a stop on the edge of the chasm. Colts blazed and bullets spanged the earth around Frank's feet as he stumbled forward. Jack pulled hard on the reins turning the horse from its forward gallop. As the horse slithered round Frank leaped up behind Jack who kicked the horse into a gallop to carry them away from the hail of lead. Brown cursed loudly continuing to fire wildly at the riders now out of range.

'Thet shore was some leap,' commented Wayman pushing his sombrero back on his head and wiping his brow. 'I guess we shore scared them hombres. They won't return to trouble us. After the way we jumped them they'll figure we've got Dan an' thet he's talked an' they'll know the game's up. C'm on let's git back to town.'

A mile away four dust-covered weary cowboys gasping for breath dropped from their horses without a word. They lay in the shelter of some rocks for a few minutes before Jack spoke.

'You shore gave us a scare, Frank. Thought for a moment you hadn't made it.'

Frank smiled weakly. 'So did I. I guess when I saw thet hole I checked the old boy slightly an' threw him off his stride. How's the shoulder Clint?'

'Mighty sore, son, but I'll be all right. There's not many round these parts thet's made thet leap. We shore scared them hombres.'

'I guess they'll figure they've run us out of

the district,' laughed Howard. 'Dan's idea worked powerful well but they shore were a big, determined bunch thet got on our tails.'

'An' they'd git a big shock if they knew who was goin' to ride back into Red Springs.'

Chapter 9

'Wal, I guess I can move my herd in peace now,' observed John Wayman as the posse headed for Red Springs.

'I think we'd better be careful, John,' answered Fennell more as a matter of form rather than a suggestion. 'I'd better arrange fer an escort fer you.'

'Nonsense, Luke,' laughed Wayman. 'We've broken up the gang. They're not likely to strike again when we've got McCoy in gaol.'

Bill Collins smiled. Dan's plan was working. Lulled into a sense of security Wayman was spurning protection and would not guard his herd against a rustling attack. With things made easy for him Wes Brown would make the most of his chances and if all went well Collins figured Dan would be on hand to follow up his plan. But Bill was puzzled by the thoughtful look on Brown's face.

'We owe you a lot, Bill,' called Wayman with a smile. 'Lucky you decided to cut across Black Ridge on your way back. You spotting thet gang saved us a lot of searchin'. What's wrong, Wes, you look troubled?'

Brown grunted. 'There's one or two things don't quite add up.'

The three cowboys looked at him sharply.

'What you mean?' asked Collins warily.

'I don't git you,' said Wayman. 'Everythin's all right.'

'Wal, we seem to hev got McCoy too easily. Why should he come into the saloon like thet?'

'Sheer bravado,' laughed Wayman. 'They're all the same, too big fer their boots. He wanted to gloat over the fact thet your scheme with Frank hadn't come off.'

'Maybe,' mused Brown. 'Another thing,' he added, 'I reckon those riders knew Death Drop Canyon an' saw it as a means of escape.'

'So what?' asked Wayman furrows wrinking his weather-beaten brow.

'Wal,' drawled Wes, 'thet could mean local men.'

Collins stared hard at Brown wishing he knew what was going on in the other man's mind.

Luke Fennell was annoyed that Brown should be advancing such theories. Everything seemed to have played into their hands and now Brown was casting suspicions into Wayman's mind. The sheriff glanced hard at the Circle C foreman. Wayman was happy to move his herd without escort and yet if Brown went much further he would have the rancher asking for one.

Suddenly Wayman laughed loudly. 'You git some queer ideas, Wes. They needn't be local men to know Death Drop Canyon. I reckon McCoy's been around here fer some time with this gang he brought from way up north. Must hev been to hev rustled those other cattle durin' the last year. Hangin' out in these hills they'd know about the Canyon.'

'I'm not so shore. I reckon Luke ought to keep careful watch on McCoy an' you'd better let the Circle C boys escort you.'

Fennell smiled as he realised Wes wanted to provide so-called protection so that he would be in the most advantageous position when he wanted to strike.

'Wouldn't hear of it, Wes,' answered the rancher. 'I'm grateful fer what you did this mornin' but I can't keep you away from your work. I'm shore you're all wrong. Nothin' can happen now we've broken up the gang.'

Brown started to protest but Wayman interrupted him. 'Don't think I don't appreciate your concern, Wes, I do, but I figure you're seein' more in this than there really is, besides what's Hiram Griffiths goin' to say if you spend your time protectin' me when there's no need?'

The dark foreman did not answer but merely shrugged his shoulders.

Half a mile further on Brown nodded to Fennell and gradually they dropped behind Wayman and Collins.

'Luke,' whispered Brown, 'be shore to keep a close watch on McCoy.'

The sheriff puckered his brow. 'You figure there'll be an attempt to rescue him?'

'Yeah. An' we don't want him out. You'll hev to be suspicious of everyone.'

Fennell stared at the cowboy by his side. 'Then you really meant what you said about them bein' local men?'

Brown nodded. 'McCoy's got someone around here who believes in him an' somehow they got wind of what we're up to, otherwise why were they out there this mornin'?'

'Could be right,' mused Fennell stroking his chin.

'There's somethin' goin' on thet I can't quite put my finger on. We got McCoy too easily an' it was rather a coincidence thet

Collins should arrive when he did AND hev seen the masked riders.'

The sheriff stared incredulously at Brown. 'You don't mean that Bill– No, thet's too fantastic.'

'Remember, McCoy was almost one of the Collins' family,' Brown reminded him.

'Wal he's not now!' shouted Fennell, anger rising in his eyes.

'Quiet,' hissed Brown. 'It's possible thet when Barbara saw him again she–'

'I don't believe it,' snapped Fennell. 'Barbara's engaged to me.'

'All right, I may be wrong but watch McCoy carefully,' warned the foreman.

'Trust me to do thet,' hissed the sheriff. 'I want him out of the way as much as you.'

'Good. Wayman won't take protection now an' I wanted to be near him to know all his moves; now we'll hev to tail him. One thing, though,' he smiled, 'he won't be expectin' rustlers so it will be easy.'

Collins noticed the two cowboys in whispered conversation but he could learn nothing as Wayman held him with talk.

'It looks as if my last three years are goin' to pay off,' mused the rancher. 'I don't mind tellin' you I got quite a scare with thet rustlin' attempt this mornin'. If thet had come off I was ruined.'

'Hiram Griffiths would probably hev bought your ranch,' commented Bill.

'Shore he would. Wanted it bad three years ago. An' a good price he offered. Wouldn't offer thet now 'cause I'd be forced to sell whatever the price. Three years ago I was prepared to go up to my neck in debt to hold the ranch; couldn't do thet agin. When I git thet herd through I'll be able to pay off all my debts an' thet'll be a day to celebrate.'

'Shore will,' smiled Bill Collins. 'I guess you'll move thet herd as soon as possible?'

'Yeah. I figure we'll spend tonight on the range an' move early in the mornin'.'

Collins eased himself in the saddle. He felt easier in his mind now that he knew when Wayman would move from the valley. As soon as the posse hit town he made his way to McCoy's home hoping that it would not be long before Clint, Frank and his sons returned.

From the gaol Dan heard the riders return but he spent a worried half hour before Luke Fennell entered his office and came along to Dan's cell.

'Wal, McCoy,' he drawled pushing his sombrero back on his head. 'We shore made them hombres of yours run. I guess they won't come back in a hurry.'

Dan smiled. 'Didn't you catch 'em Fennell?' he mocked.

'No, but what odds? We got you an' we ran 'em far enough. They wouldn't hev got away but fer a mad leap over Death Drop Canyon.'

'What!' gasped Dan.

'Yeah. I shore got to hand it to your riders they shore know how to handle horseflesh.' He leaned against the bars. 'Wal, McCoy, looks like the end of the trail fer you fer some years.'

'Ain't you goin' to give Wayman more protection?'

'No need now we hev you here,' grinned the sheriff as he turned away from the cell.

'Needs protection from Wes Brown!' said Dan quietly.

Fennell swung round startled.

'What you mean, McCoy?' he snapped.

'You know what I mean,' drawled Dan. 'You know I didn't try to rustle them cattle. We were there 'cause we overheard your arrangements with Brown.'

Fennell looked suspiciously at Dan. 'You couldn't,' he muttered.

'Shore we did. You were followed to thet hut.'

The sheriff gasped. He glared at Dan. 'You

seem to know too much fer the good of your health, McCoy,' he hissed angrily.

'Don't be a fool, Fennell. Pull out an' square yourself with the law before it's too late.'

Anger disappeared from Luke's face as a grin broadened across his lips. 'It's you thet's the fool. The cards are stacked agin you an' you're in safe hands.' He turned and walked quickly to his office.

Dan watched the door close behind him. He had failed in his attempt to split Fennell from Brown so all he could do was to wait for his friends to carry out their part of his plan.

Bill Collins climbed wearily from his horse outside McCoy's house. The chase had tired him. Suddenly he felt his age, and realised he was no longer as young as he used to be. But he was determined to see this thing through. He had sided with McCoy although the sign of cowardice had been strong against him. He liked the young ex-sheriff and when he saw that Barbara accepted Dan's story he had followed suit. He wanted happiness for his daughter and although there was something about Fennell which he did not like, if he was the man she wanted then he accepted her decision. However with the return of

Dan McCoy he had noticed a change in Barbara and as events had unfolded he had determined to sort right from wrong.

Barbara greeted him, her pretty face creased by a worried frown.

'What happened, Dad? I've been worried to death. Is everything all right?' she asked brushing back the curl which slipped on to her forehead.

Collins dropped on to a chair, took off his Stetson and wearily rubbed his hand across his brow.

'Yes, Babs, everythin' has gone accordin' to plan.'

The girl's eyes brightened. 'Good. Then what's wrong?'

'Nothin' really. I'm jest gettin' too old fer this sort of game, lass.'

'Nonsense,' answered Barbara brightly. 'A good cup of coffee will soon put you right.'

'Aye, happen it will. How's Mrs McCoy?'

'I think she's feelin' better now Frank's seen reason.'

'Good.'

'Put your feet up, Dad, and tell me what happened. The coffee will soon be ready.'

By the time he had finished his story and had enjoyed two cups of coffee Bill Collins was feeling much better.

'There's nothin' I can do until the others return but there's somethin' you can do Babs.'

'What's that, Dad? I'll do anything to help,' she said eagerly.

'I want you to go to see Dan an' tell him everythin' is all right. It shouldn't be hard fer you to persuade Luke to let you see him,' he added with a grin.

Barbara blushed, picked up her shawl and wrapped it round her shoulders. Collins smiled as he watched his daughter view herself in the mirror and put her hair into the position she wanted it.

'Who's this fer?' he teased. 'Dan or Luke?'

The pretty girl ignored the remark and went to the door.

'Jest a minute, Babs.' Her father halted her. 'Tell Dan that Wayman moves his herd in the morning so we'll make the rescue attempt as soon as we know he's on the move. Better tell him thet I'm a bit suspicious of Brown an' Fennell; they might be up to somethin' so as soon as the others git back someone will be close to the gaol all the time in case anythin' goes wrong.'

Barbara nodded, left the house and made her way to the sheriff's office.

Luke Fennell leaped to his feet when he

saw Barbara enter his office.

'Hello, Barbara, this is a pleasant surprise.' He moved round his desk to greet her with a kiss. 'I'm sorry I couldn't git to see you last night but my protectin' job paid dividends. We've got the rustler an' run his gang out of the district.'

'I know, Luke. I've come to see Dan,' answered Barbara coolly.

'What! Come to see Dan? But why?' Jealousy flared up in the sheriff.

'I've just come to tell him how his Ma is,' replied the girl quietly. 'I thought he ought to know that she's comfortable but worried about him.'

'Wal, I can't let you see him.'

'Now, Luke,' said Barbara coyly, 'you wouldn't refuse me, would you?' She moved closer to him.

'I'm sorry, I can't let you go to him. Wes Brown figures thet his gang is made up of local men an' I'm not letting McCoy come into contact with anyone.'

'But I'm a woman. You can't suspect me,' protested Barbara.

'No, of course I don't, darling, but you were engaged to him once an' Brown thinks your father may be mixed up in this.'

Barbara stared incredulously at Luke. Her

141

face reddened slowly. 'Luke do you follow everythin' Brown says?' Her eyes flushed with anger. 'My father's one of the most respected men in this town, you don't think he would help a rustler.'

Luke started to protest but Barbara stopped him. 'You know full well he's just come in after helping you chase the rustlers.'

'I know, Barbara. I didn't say I suspected him. It was Wes Brown.'

'Wes Brown! Are you tied to his horse saddle,' mocked Barbara. 'Can't you stand on your own feet.'

Luke turned away under the scathing words.

'No one's seein' McCoy,' he said over his shoulder.

Barbara pouted. Her eyes lost their anger. She gripped his arms and turned him round. Fingering his shirt collar she said quietly, 'I'm sorry, Luke. I lost my temper but that accusation–' She pressed herself close to him. 'I only want to tell him about his Ma.' She looked up at him with wide eyes. His arms encircled her waist. Slowly she raised herself on her toes and put her lips to his. Luke pulled her to him. A moment later she pushed him slowly away and said, 'Now, Luke, let me see him.'

The sheriff smiled at her. 'All right,' he drawled picking up a bunch of keys from his desk. 'Only a few minutes,' he warned as she stepped past him into the cell block.

Dan jumped to his feet when he saw them.

'Hello, Babs,' he called.

'Hello, Dan,' answered Barbara. 'You all right?'

'Shore, fine.'

Barbara turned to the sheriff. 'Aren't you going to let a lady in so's she can sit down!'

Reluctantly Fennell opened the cell door.

As he relocked the door he heard someone enter his office. A look of annoyance crossed his face at the interruption. He glared jealously at Dan.

'I'll be back in a few moments,' he snapped as he turned to the door.

As the sheriff left the cell block Barbara grasped Dan's hands. 'Listen carefully,' she whispered. 'He'll soon be back.' Quickly she related her father's story and passed on his message.

'Good,' commented Dan, relief in his voice. 'Tell him I'll be ready.'

'Do be careful, Dan.' Barbara looked pleadingly at the handsome cowboy by her side. 'I don't want to lose you again.'

Dan glanced at her keenly. His heart

143

pounded. 'How do you mean thet Babs?' he asked quietly.

'Only one way, Dan,' she whispered. 'I misjudged you three years ago, I want to take up where we left off.'

'Barbara!' Dan grasped the girl in his arms. 'But what about Luke?'

'I realise now that I never really loved him. I suppose I turned to someone to try to forget you.'

'You'll never hev to forgit me agin,' he whispered. Their lips met to wipe out three years of bitter memories.

'Barbara!'

The young couple were startled by the shout. They spun round to see Fennell standing in the doorway. He scowled angrily his face dark with hate. He drew his Colt as he crossed to the bars. Barbara looked startled as he flung open the door.

'Get out,' he snapped at the girl.

She looked at Dan finding reassurance in his calm and passive face. 'Do as he says, Barbara,' he said quietly.

'But – but he might kill you,' she said.

'He won't do thet,' replied Dan coolly. 'A sheriff shootin' an unarmed man in his cell is likely to lose his job.'

'Thet's right.' A voice came from the doorway. They turned to see Wes Brown smiling grimly.

Luke, fuming with rage, glared at Dan. Suddenly he slipped his Colt back into its holster, turned and followed Barbara to the office.

Without a word she picked up her basket from the desk but paused as she opened the street door and turned to Luke.

'I'm sorry,' she said. 'But it's better you know now that I'll not marry you. It's Dan I love.'

Before Fennell could reply she stepped out on to the sidewalk. As the door closed Fennell crashed his fist on the desk and cursed loudly. Brown's eyes narrowed.

'Thought I told you no one was to see McCoy,' he snapped.

'Wal, I reckoned Barbara would be all right,' answered the sheriff weakly. 'She only wanted to tell him how his Ma is.'

'That's all,' sneered Brown. 'It looks like it doesn't it?'

Fennell glared at the Circle C foreman. He shrugged his shoulders. 'Wal, maybe thet was all, what else could she possibly hev come fer?'

'She's Collins' daughter isn't she?' snapped Brown. 'You shouldn't hev let her near McCoy.'

'Aw, pack it in, Wes. You're way off beam there. Collins can't hev anythin' to do with this bunch. Your imagination's gettin' too wild.'

'Maybe, maybe not,' mused Brown. He laid his hand on Fennell's shoulder. 'Now fergit her Luke an' concentrate on the job on hand. When thet comes off you'll git such a packet thet any gal in town will be glad to marry the fine upright sheriff whose maiden aunt back east has left him a fortune.' He laughed loud as he slapped Luke on the back and strode to the door.

Fennell glared at the foreman's back but his thoughts were rudely interrupted as the door burst open almost knocking the Circle C foreman over.

A young, hatless cowboy, his clothes torn and dusty, his face bleeding, gasped as he stumbled into the office.

'Quick, sheriff,' he panted. 'Over to the saloon; there's hell on.' He turned as he saw Wes. 'You'd better go too, Brown, they're your polecats that's beatin' my buddies up.'

Brown and Fennell ran from the office, crossed the dusty road and crashed open the batwings to see Butch, Al and their cronies beating up two cowboys in a corner.

146

Fennell looked sharply at Brown who nodded. The sheriff drew his Colt from its leather and fired over the heads of the fighters. The explosion startled the cowboys. The Circle C men spun round and the other two slowly picked themselves up from the floor.

'Break it up,' snapped Fennell. 'The next ounce of lead might hev someone's name on it. Right, who started this?'

The youngster who had called the sheriff spoke up. 'They did. We were jest havin' a quiet drink when these coyotes wanted the table, said they always sat there.'

'I've warned you about this before,' snapped Brown glaring at his cowpokes. 'Save your fightin' fer the proper time. Goin' to run 'em in sheriff?'

'Naw, but will next time.' He looked across at Blackie behind the bar. 'What's the damage, Blackie?' he called.

'Aw, I dunno, 'bout forty dollars I reckon.'

'Right, thet's ten dollars each fer you Circle C mugs. Over to the bar an' pay up.' He motioned with his Colt. The four cowboys shuffled over to the counter and reluctantly threw the bills in front of Blackie.

'Git back to the Circle C,' ordered Brown. 'I'll see you out there.' He turned to Fennell. 'Drink, Luke?'

'Thanks,' muttered Luke. 'Be with you in a minute. I'll jest see this bunch off the premises.' He followed Butch and his side-kicks out of the saloon glad that they had created a disturbance for it had given him an idea.

As the four cowpokes swung into the saddles Luke leaned on the rail watching Butch carefully.

'Hold it,' he called as the four men turned their mounts. Fennell stepped off the side-walk and moved close to Butch's saddle. 'How'd you like to git your own back on McCoy?' he asked quietly.

'You know the answer to thet,' muttered Butch drawing his hairy hand across his mouth. 'But you got him all locked up nice an' safe.'

'So what?' answered Luke. 'Listen care-fully an' you'll git paid fer your pleasure.'

Butch leaned forward in the saddle. A few minutes later four cowboys rode out of Red Springs whilst Fennell joined Brown at the bar.

Chapter 10

Barbara found her father refreshed from a short sleep and eager for news of Dan. The girl told her story quickly.

Bill Collins frowned as he paced the floor. 'A man jealous in love is dangerous an' there's no tellin' what Luke might git up to. I wish Clint and the boys would hurry up. We must git outside that gaol as soon as possible.'

It was a worried hour before the four riders returned. As they washed and refreshed themselves Bill Collins acquainted them of the latest facts. With these in mind they reformed their plans.

After the hard ride Clint's wound bothered him and reluctantly he agreed to stay at McCoy's house.

'You never know if Luke may try to git at Dan through Barbara,' pointed out Collins, 'and it would be as well fer one of us to be around, besides as we are goin' to split up it may be useful to have one person in a set place, ready to aid either party.'

As soon as all was ready Frank McCoy and Jack Collins rode out of town to the ranges beyond the Wayman ranch to keep watch on the herd and any movements which Wes Brown might make.

Bill Collins accompanied by Howard walked to the main street where they strolled casually along the sidewalk keeping a watchful eye on the sheriff's office.

The town was beginning to awake from the fierce heat of the early afternoon. Father and son reclined in the chairs outside the hotel, talking to acquaintances and idling the remainder of the afternoon watching the life of Red Springs pass by, but always watching the office of the lawman across the street. The afternoon turned into evening but still nothing happened to arouse the suspicions of either Bill Collins or his son. Bill felt happier as the time went by. Maybe he was being over cautious; maybe Fennell wasn't up to any tricks.

The sun dropped lower in the west; darkness began to fall across the town and the night wind sent a chill flurry through the dust of Main Street, Red Springs, Texas. Two cowboys still kept watch. The night life of the town stirred as cowboys rode in to enjoy a rest from the day's work. Howard eyed each group carefully as they passed. The noise from the saloon grew louder; the occasional drunk floundered across the street; cowpunchers with their wives rode by in buggies to visit friends; cowboys with a girl on their arm sauntered past; groups leaned on the rails yarning; the night life of Red Springs was normal. The night wore on, gradually took command and the noise of the town subsided. Cowpokes rode back to their ranches; town-dwellers made their way home whilst others found a place for the night.

Howard dozed. His father was beginning to think that they were keeping a useless vigil when suddenly he was aware that there was something odd about the street. He puzzled over it but couldn't decide what was different. For the fifth time he glanced along the street noting every detail. His gaze moved past the sheriff's office and on to the hardware store. Suddenly he stiffened. There it was; it had been opposite to him all the time and because he had expected it he had not really noticed it. A light still gleamed from the sheriff's office whereas normally Luke had left long before this.

Collins sat upright in his chair, tense, alert, his head inclined towards the south, listening. He nudged his son, silencing him with a guarded whisper and nodded in the direction of the faint sound of approaching horses. They were being ridden at a slow walk, their hoofs clopping on the hard road under the dust. He had no reason to be suspicious but Bill Collins felt that something was going to happen, that this was what they had been waiting for. He motioned to his son. They pushed themselves out of the chairs and shrank into the shadows of the hotel. Both automatically checked the hang of their Colts and eased them in their holsters. Gradually four riders appeared out of the darkness. Bill Collins drew a sharp breath when he noticed they had a spare horse ready saddled.

'Butch and his cronies,' whispered Howard.

His father nodded.

The riders halted before the sheriff's office, swung slowly out of their saddles, paused to glance up and down the street before moving swiftly to the office door and stepping swiftly inside.

'C'm on,' whispered Bill, his voice cool but urgent.

Father and son hurried quickly across the street. They stepped carefully on to the sidewalk, making no noise, and slid into the shadows alongside the office window. Cautiously they peered inside.

Luke Fennell was seated at his desk, his hands raised above his head. The four Circle C men had Colts in their hands and watched Luke carefully.

'Git the keys, Al,' ordered Butch.

The stubble-chinned Al grinned as he picked up the keys and crossed the room to the door leading to the cells.

'I shore is goin' to enjoy this,' he laughed.

'Shut up,' snapped Butch. 'Jes git on with it.'

Howard gripped his father's arm. 'C'm on,' he whispered. 'They'll kill Dan.'

Collins restrained his son. 'No,' he answered. 'They've got a spare horse. They mean to take Dan fer a ride. Let them git Dan out fer us.' He pulled his neckerchief over the lower half of his face and Howard followed suit.

A few moments later Dan appeared pushed forward by Al's Colt.

'Here he is, Butch,' Al rasped.

'I cin see,' hissed the leader. 'You talk too much, Al.' He glanced hatefully at Dan before turning to the sheriff. 'Don't attempt to follow us, Fennell, one of my boys will be watchin'.'

Luke grinned to himself. Butch knew he would never attempt to do that but he was certainly making it sound realistic.

'Right, McCoy, move. This is the end of the road fer you,' ordered Butch as he motioned towards the door with his guns.

Dan hesitated.

In that moment Bill Collins leaped for the door and flung it open. Every man in the room gasped when they saw the two masked men. Butch, snarling like an animal at bay, deprived of something he wanted, swung his guns round. Bill's Colt spat. Butch gasped, doubled up and fired as he fell to the floor but his bullets ground harmlessly into the floorboards. Bill's left hand hurled death towards one of the sidekicks who yelled as the lead smashed his chest. As he stepped through the door Howard shouted 'Catch, Dan!' and threw the gun in his left hand to his friend who caught it neatly as he sprang towards Fennell. The sheriff had leaped to his feet but everything happened so quickly that his gun had not left its holster before Dan was beside him with a Colt sticking in his ribs.

'Leave it, Fennell,' he hissed.

The Colt in Howard's right hand fired rapidly and Al dropped to the floor, the look of surprise frozen to his face as he pitched forward. The fourth cowboy, shaken by the suddenness of the attack, fired wildly but his gun was silenced as Howard's bullet shattered his wrist. His gun clattered to the floor and he sank against the wall yelling with pain.

'Shore glad to see you,' grinned Dan flinging Fennell's guns on to the desk.

''fraid we hed to move in sooner than we planned with these hombres breezin' in.'

'Can't be helped,' said Dan. 'Glad you followed up your suspicions.'

Yells came from outside as the few cowboys left in the saloon ran across the street.

'Quick,' ordered Dan. 'Off with those masks. You've jest stopped these coyotes from takin' me. Make thet hombre tell why they did. Here's your gun, Howard.'

Bill Collins grasped Dan's plan and nodded approval. They pulled down their neckerchiefs.

'Collins!' gasped Fennell. 'I might hev known,' he added weakly. Anger and hate stirred within him. 'You'll not git away with it,' he hissed.

'Keep your mouth shut,' snapped Bill moving threateningly with his gun.

The door burst open and the cowboys

came abruptly to a halt at the scene which met them.

Collins spoke up quickly. 'Jest prevented Butch an' his Circle C cronies from takin' McCoy. Thet polecat might tell us what they were up to.'

Howard moved across to the frightened cowboy nursing his wrist.

'Wal?' he snapped. 'Talk!'

The cowboy glanced sharply at Fennell and tightened his lips.

'Talk!' repeated Howard and crashed his Colt on to the shattered wrist.

The cowboy yelled with pain.

'There's more if you don't talk,' informed young Collins. He raised his hand menacingly.

'No, not agin,' shouted the Circle C man. Sweat stood on his forehead; his eyes filled with fear. 'I'll talk. It was him.' He pointed at Fennell. 'He put us up to it.'

The sheriff opened his mouth to speak but he saw Bill's Colt move persuadingly and his eyes flashed a warning. Fennell closed his mouth knowing that Collins would not hesitate to press the trigger.

'What do you mean?' queried Howard.

'He wanted McCoy out of the way 'cause his girl threw him up fer McCoy.' The words came reluctantly from between clenched teeth. 'He got us to fake this hold-up an' we were to take McCoy fer a ride.'

A murmur ran through the cowboys crowding the door.

Before anyone could speak Bill Collins took command of the situation. 'I'll put McCoy back where he belongs an' these other two with him. Some of you clear up this mess.'

Cowboys shuffled forward to do his bidding. He was respected in Red Springs and no one questioned his authority. Howard and his father prodded the three cowboys forward to the cells. When they returned to the office the bodies had been carried out.

'We'll need someone to take over here fer the time being,' Collins called to the waiting cowpokes. 'I suggest we git Clint Schofield back in harness; he'll know the run of things.'

Murmured approval came from the group.

'All right, then thet's settled,' continued Bill. 'You can all go home now an' Howard you fetch Clint. I'll hang on here until you git back.'

Cowboys shuffled away from the office and Howard hurried with the news to Clint. Bill flopped into a chair as the door closed.

A deep sigh escaped from his pale lips. It had been a tricky situation but everything had worked out all right thanks to Dan's quick thinking and his own handling of the situation.

About twenty minutes elapsed before Howard returned with Clint.

'You shore hev hed a clean up,' grinned Clint as Bill climbed out of the chair to greet him.

'Yeah. Things got a bit tricky when the cowpokes from the saloon headed here but we got over thet one, an' with their approval you're to take charge here fer the time bein'.'

'Good. It'll be a pleasure to keep my eye on thet coyote, Fennell, after he kicked me out of my job.' Clint automatically checked the hang of his guns as if anticipating action. 'Reckon the first job of the temporary sheriff is to release the innocent party.' He picked up the keys from the desk and strode to the cells.

'Sorry I hed to leave you there, Dan,' apologised Collins as the young cowboy walked into the office. 'I reckoned it best in case any of them thar cowpokes returned and got inquisitive.'

'Shore was all right,' grinned Dan. 'You

were mighty quick on the uptake an' now Clint tells me you got those folk to agree to him acting as sheriff.'

Bill nodded. 'Reckoned it would suit us fine to hev him in here.'

Dan agreed. 'Think you'll be all right with that arm of yours?' he asked.

'Shore, son,' drawled the old man. 'If I cin jump Death Drop Canyon with one good arm then I figure I cin handle a Colt. Besides, I'd manage anything to see you back here as sheriff.'

Dan grinned and patted Clint on the shoulder. 'Thanks, Clint, an' when I'm back here you'll be with me.' He picked up the star lying on the desk where Collins had thrown it after ripping it from Fennell's shirt. 'Reckon we'd better make this official, like.'

Clint stuck his chest out proudly as Dan pinned the badge to his shirt.

The brief ceremony over Dan became deadly serious as they sat down.

'We'll hev to sit tight until we hear from Jack and Frank. Then we go into action an' if all goes well we should clear things up very soon. Bill, I'd like you to stay here with Clint; he may need some help an' if things get a bit sticky then you can git after us.'

Bill nodded and lit his pipe.

Dan turned to Clint. 'I don't know how long we'll be, Clint, might be a few days. D'you reckon you can hang on to them hombres 'till we git back?'

'Shore we will, eh Bill?' asserted Clint.

Collins nodded again without speaking.

'Good,' approved Dan. 'Howard, you an' I will leave as soon as we git word from the others. See that the horses are ready an' we've kit fer a few days ride.'

'Right, Dan,' said Howard, shoving himself out of a chair. He left the office and was not long before he was back to report all was ready at the back of the building.

'Are you goin' to jump Wes Brown as he moves in?' asked Clint stroking his chin.

'No,' drawled Dan. 'I'm goin' to let Brown git those cattle but I want to be on hand when he does.'

The three cowboys stared at Dan as he announced this unexpected idea.

'I'm sorry for Wayman, it'll upset his arrangements, but he'll git his cattle back.' Dan smiled as he saw surprise on the faces of his companions. He swung back in his chair. 'You see I'm goin' to play a hunch; I figure there are bigger brains behind this than Wes Brown.' He paused and leaned forward on the desk. He looked keenly at each of the three cowboys in turn. 'Just one thing more, Wes Brown is my man; I've an old score to settle with him an' if I git my way it'll be settled outside thet door in front of the townsfolk.'

Chapter 11

The first grey streaks of dawn broadened on the eastern sky. The light spread, spilled into Red Springs and crept through the windows into the sheriff's office. Dan stirred in his hard chair. He stretched his long powerful frame, blinked at the strengthening light and looked round the room.

Clint, who had kept watch through the remaining hours of darkness, smiled. 'Wal, son, guess you'd better be gittin' ready.'

Dan nodded, pushed himself out of the chair and shook Bill Collins and Howard. After a hasty breakfast Howard grabbed his Stetson.

'Reckon I'd better git outside. Frank or Jack'll wonder what's happened if they don't see any of us about.'

He stepped outside, leaned on the rail and anxiously watched the south road.

The sun crept slowly above the horizon and a lone cowboy lashed his horse towards the town. Howard stirred, narrowed his eyes and gazed at the cloud of dust. Long before he could make out the rider's features he recognised his brother from the way he sat his horse.

'Jack's comin'!' he called through the doorway and turned back to the street.

Jack slowed his sweating horse to a walk as he entered the town and eagerly looked around for his father and brother. He was surprised when he saw Howard move from the rail outside the sheriff's office and step down into the dust of the road.

'Don't look alarmed,' grinned Howard as Jack pulled his horse to a halt. 'Butch an' his sidekicks tried to git Dan an' we hed to move in sooner than we expected.'

'Everythin' all right?' asked Jack anxiously as he swung out of the saddle.

'Shore,' replied Howard. 'Butch, Al an' one of the pokes won't talk again. We hev the other an' Fennell in gaol.'

The two brothers hurried into the office where quick greetings were exchanged.

'Wayman's on the move,' Jack announced.

'Good,' said Dan. 'Any sign of Brown?'

'Nope,' answered Jack taking the cup of coffee which his father handed to him.

'Wal, I reckon he won't strike until Wayman's through the hills,' drawled Dan. 'Where did you leave Frank?'

'Up at Smokey Rocks,' replied Jack. 'We're to meet him there.'

'Right,' said Dan picking up his Stetson. 'We'll hit the trail. Ready Howard?'

'Yes,' answered the young cowboy hitching up his belt. 'Jack, our horses are at the back, see you there.'

Jack nodded, finished his drink and left the office.

Dan turned to his two friends. 'So long, Clint. So long, Bill. Thanks fer what you're doin'.'

'So long, son. Look out fer Brown,' advised Clint, his brown, contoured face serious as he held out his hand.

'Take care of yourself, Dan. I know Babs will be anxious.' Collins' face was grave. 'We'll be watchin' fer you.'

Dan smiled, swung on his heels and left the office. Howard followed him and as they swung into their saddles Jack joined them. The three cowboys left Red Springs, put their horses into a long steady lope and headed for the hills.

They made good progress and in less than an hour they were riding along the hill top towards Frank's lookout. They slipped from their horses and joined Frank amongst the rocks.

'Everythin' normal when Wayman moved off,' he reported. 'He had no extra spread men so it'll be a cinch fer Brown when he strikes.'

'Any sign of him?' asked Dan.

'No.'

The herd was a few miles down the valley and moving at a steady pace. Dan narrowed his eyes and watched it for a few moments without speaking. The riders were keeping the cattle in a compact group and the stragglers were being promptly shepherded back to the herd by the dragmen.

Dan turned to his three companions. 'I reckon we'll stick to the hills at this side. If Wayman takes the trail through Longhorn Gulch, an' I reckon he will, then we'll out-ride him, cross the valley an' then through the hills to a point above the Gulch where Starlight Canyon runs into it.'

The Collins brothers murmured their approval.

'Good idea,' said Jack. 'I reckon Wayman will halt fer the night in the Gulch. He'll hev better control of the cattle there.'

'C'm on then, let's go,' Dan ordered. The cowboys sprang into the saddles and followed the herd at a steady pace.

They rode all morning and well into the

afternoon until Dan saw the point riders and swingmen gently but firmly turn the herd across the valley towards Longhorn Gulch which cut through the hills to the rolling country stretching north to the railhead. Dan kept to the hill top but passed beyond the herd before pulling his horse to a halt.

'Reckon we can stop here a while an' hev some grub. It'll take them some time to git the herd into the Gulch.'

They welcomed the relief from the saddle, and prepared a meal of beef and beans, with hot coffee to swill it down. They kept a careful watch on the distant herd but saw nothing unusual.

When the dragmen had moved out of sight into the Gulch they swung into the saddles and sent their horses in a twisting, slithering, slide, down the hillside. Once they reached the valley Dan quickened the pace, eager to outride Wayman's outfit and position himself at the junction of Longhorn Gulch and Starlight Canyon.

The sun was lowering to the western horizon as they gained the hills and urged their horses up the slope. They threaded their way through the scrub, twisted and turned above the Gulch and reached the desired vantage point before dark.

Howard took the four horses and settled them for the night close to some sheltering rocks whilst Frank prepared the camp in a small hollow. Dan and Jack hurried to the edge of the hill and keeping down out of sight watched Wayman's outfit settled for the night.

'Guess Brown'll take this herd at the far end of the Gulch,' muttered Jack.

Dan nodded in agreement.

'C'm on let's go fer some grub, guess Frank'll hev it ready.' Jack was about to jump to his feet when Dan's hand halted him.

'Keep down,' he whispered.

Jack flattened himself turning his head towards Dan. 'What's wrong?' he asked quietly.

'Someone over there,' answered Dan nodding towards the hill on the far side of Starlight Canyon.

Jack followed his gaze but could see nothing except a dark hillside.

'You shore?' he whispered.

'A sombrero broke the skyline fer a fraction of a second. If I hedn't been lookin' in that particular spot I'd never hev seen it.'

'Lucky fer us,' replied Jack. 'Maybe Brown's goin' to move in sooner than we expect.'

167

Dan nudged Jack. 'C'm on, an' keep right down.'

The two cowboys crept Indian fashion to the hollow where they found a meal awaiting them.

After Dan had related their observations Frank was the first to speak.

'Could be a wanderin' cowboy.'

'Then he'd hev no need to be creepin' about,' pointed out Dan, 'an' if he hadn't been creepin' more than a sombrero would hev broken the skyline.'

'Reckon it could be a lookout man from Brown's gang,' commented Howard.

'Shore,' agreed Jack. 'Brown would never jump Wayman's herd in the Gulch. It'd be slower to git the cattle on the move an' too easy fer Wayman to strike back. What you think, Dan?'

Dan looked thoughtful. 'Could be right,' he muttered. His brow furrowed. 'Supposin' Brown's goin' to rustle them here an' not take them through the Gulch?'

His companions were startled by this remark.

'What do you mean?' asked Frank. 'He can't take them anywhere else.'

'Can't he?' drawled Dan. 'What about Starlight Canyon?'

'Starlight Canyon!' gasped Jack. 'What's the point? He can't git the cattle out at the other end.'

'You shore?' queried Dan shaking himself a smoke.

'Wal, I suppose he could, but it'd require all his skill an' it wouldn't be the quick getaway of a rustler.'

'Time doesn't matter to Brown so long as Wayman can't follow him immediately.'

'Wal, he could up there.'

'Not if Brown makes it too hot fer him.'

'I get it,' said Frank excitedly. 'A few well-armed men at the entrance to the Canyon would keep Wayman back.'

Dan nodded. 'Thet's right.'

'I think you've got it!' exclaimed Howard. 'Brown's tested this route with these smaller rustlin's thet hev been goin' on ready fer the big move.'

'Shore,' continued Frank eagerly. 'A big herd would be difficult but he could hold off pursuers long enough to get it well away.'

'Wait until they git in the Canyon an' then slaughter them more likely,' muttered Jack, 'an' then no one could follow 'em. You've got to hand it to Brown fer ideas.'

'Maybe not Brown,' said Dan thoughtfully.

'What are we goin' to do now, Dan?' asked Frank. 'We can't let Wayman's cowpokes git slaughtered jest fer the sake of us followin' Brown.'

'We could be wrong,' pointed out Jack. 'Brown maybe won't jump the herd here.'

'I know,' said Dan. 'But we can't take any risk; we must suppose he is.' He paused a moment, frowning at his thoughts. 'Look, I reckon we're forced into the open with Wayman an' he'll either hev to trust us or see his cowpokes shot down.'

'But if we interfere now it'll give the game away to Brown,' said Howard.

'Wal, maybe not but we'll hev to alter our plans. Now listen, I reckon we might play it this way.'

Dan discussed his ideas with his companions before they made their final plan.

Wayman's efficient cowboys soon had things ready for the night halt. Weary men tumbled from their saddles, turned their horses over to two of their companions and eagerly waded into the steaming stew prepared by the chuck waggon team. Once Wayman had decided who was to watch the herd during the night the others enjoyed a smoke before turning in. After a day in the saddle sleep

170

came easily to the entire outfit. Assuring himself that all was well John Wayman rolled himself in his blankets and settled down to sleep close to the chuck waggon.

An hour passed; all was quiet in the sleeping camp. The flames from the fire flickered lower and lower and now only occasionally leaped to send a faint light across the still figures around it.

Two shadowy forms slid cautiously down the hillside. With Colts drawn they crept stealthily towards the sleeping figures. They moved through the camp silently examining the sleeping men until they came to Wayman. The masked men looked at each other and nodded. They slipped their guns back into their holsters and the shorter of the two untied a second neckerchief from around his throat. He bent over the sleeping figure and before Wayman knew what was happening a gag was tied round his mouth stifling all attempts to shout. Powerful hands grabbed his arms, dragged him to his feet, and bundled him quickly round the chuck waggon away from the camp.

Eyes wide with astonishment Wayman twisted in a useless attempt to escape. He felt hard steel rammed into his back and a voice hissed 'No noise!' He was bundled unceremoniously up the hillside hoping the camp would suddenly burst into life, but all was silent behind them.

No one spoke as they reached the top of the hill. The masked men bustled him forward before turning left and heading for a group of rocks.

It was only when they dropped into a hollow that Wayman noticed a fire screened by the rocks. His captors pushed him forward towards it. He stopped and gasped with surprise when the glow revealed Frank McCoy and Howard Collins sitting against a rock.

His escort stopped beside him.

'No hollerin' when we take this gag off,' warned the taller cowboy.

The gag was slipped from his face and he swung round to face the two cowboys. A long breath of amazement escaped from his lips as they removed the neckerchiefs from their faces.

'McCoy! How the hell did you git here? Jack, what are you doin' with this here rustler?'

'Come over by the fire an' hev a cup of coffee.' Dan's voice was friendly. 'We hev a lot of talkin' to do.'

'Like hell we hev,' stormed the rancher

172

whose black look bored into Dan.

Dan's eyes narrowed. 'Wayman, it's fer your own good. Jack an' I hed to git you up here an' we knew you wouldn't come of your own free will. I'm sorry fer the way we did it but–' Dan shrugged his shoulders. 'It was necessary.'

'I reckon thet now you're here you may as well hear what we hev to say,' said Jack. 'As Dan says it's fer your own good.'

'I'll bet it is,' muttered Wayman sarcastically, as he stepped forward and sat down close to the fire. He took the mug of coffee, offered by Frank, with murmured thanks. He sipped at it whilst he glanced over the mug at each of the cowboys in turn.'

'I don't git it,' he said. 'What's it all about? What are you doin' up here?'

'All in good time, Mr Wayman,' smiled Dan, 'but let's begin at the beginning.' Dan related the events of the past two days and explained his suspicions and theories.

'Wal,' drawled the rancher when Dan finished. 'You make it sound mighty convincin' but I've nothin' to make me suspicious, only against you. Why didn't you come to me before instead of stampedin' the herd?'

'You wouldn't hev believed me if I hed. Remember you packed me off your ranch at

173

the point of a gun an' as you say there was nothin' to make you suspicious of Wes Brown – his cowhands were helpin' Fennell to guard your herd.'

Wayman nodded. Suddenly he eyed Dan suspiciously. 'How do I know this isn't a trick?'

'Look, Wayman,' pointed out Dan. 'You've got to trust me an' I've got to trust you. I'm lettin' you go back to camp an' there'll be nothin' to stop you comin' after us but I reckon you won't. Your curiosity's raised about this other possibility. If nothin' happens then you'll drive your herd on down the Gulch but if somethin' does happen–'

'Then we'll be ready fer 'em,' broke in Wayman. 'Right, McCoy, I'll trust you.' He started to get to his feet but Jack stopped him.

'It's not quite as simple as thet,' he drawled.

'Now what?' Suspicion sprang into the rancher's voice.

Dan's face wore a serious mask. 'Wal, Mr Wayman, I'm goin' to ask you to let Brown rustle thet herd if he attempts it.'

'What!' yelled Wayman. 'I guessed you'd be up to some trickery.'

'No tricks,' went on Dan quietly. 'With the

tip off we've given you, presumin' we're right, then you could save the herd but thet wouldn't git the rustlers. You'd hev no proof thet it was Wes Brown thet tried to rustle your cattle an' he'd be left to strike again.'

Wayman grunted. He knew Dan was right.

The young cowboy pressed his case. 'Let Brown git your herd; let your cowpokes fake the attempt to follow them so as to make it look real an' you be up here to trail Brown with us.'

'We can jump him higher up the Canyon an' catch him red-handed.'

Dan smiled and shook his head. Wayman looked puzzled, frowning beneath the brim of his sombrero.

'I want to trail Brown to see where he takes these cattle. I figure there's someone bigger behind all this.' Wayman shot a sharp glance at Dan. 'I may be wrong about all this, Mr Wayman, but will you play along?'

The cattleman did not answer immediately. He glanced at the cowboys one by one. Each pair of eyes was riveted on him waiting expectantly. The fire glowed on grim unmoving countenances.

Wayman drew a deep breath. 'I guess so,' he whispered.

The tension broke as each cowboy relaxed.

'But see here, McCoy,' went on Wayman, 'an' you others, if you're pullin' a fast one I'll hound you down an' kill you with my own hands.' He pushed himself to his feet. 'I'll be back before sun-up,' he added curtly. He stepped out of the fire-light and disappeared into the darkness.

The sharp bite of pre-dawn cold was still in the air when Frank McCoy hurried from the look-out point into the camp to wake his sleeping companions.

'Time to git ready,' he called. As the three cowboys tumbled out of their blankets he nodded towards the Gulch. 'Nothin' happenin' out there yet,' he informed them.

They were enjoying their breakfast when the faint clop of a horse made them drop their forks and draw their Colts. They waited expectantly, eyes piercing the gloom.

'All right,' whispered Dan as the shadowy figure became more distinct. 'It's Wayman.'

The rancher swung from his horse and wished them a curt 'Good morning.'

'Frank, Howard, clear up here an' git everythin' ready to move.'

The two cowboys nodded and finished

176

their meal hastily.

Dan turned to Wayman. 'You tell your men Mr Wayman?'

'Shore, they're ready for anythin'.' His voice was sharp and Dan sensed that he still had his doubts about the whole affair.

'Good. You come with Jack an' me, we'll keep our eyes on things below.'

They hurried to the edge of the hill and laid down to await events.

The low moan of cattle rose and fell on the gentle breeze. Light from the eastern horizon began to creep along the hill-tops and slowly penetrate the darkened Gulch. Suddenly Jack leaned forward. He signalled to his companions and pointed to the foot of the hill. Two shadowy figures crept stealthily towards the horses tethered a short distance from the camp. Swiftly and silently they released the horses and sent them galloping away from the camp towards the Canyon.

Wayman gasped. 'You're right, Dan. The herd's at his mercy now; I've the minimum of riders out with the herd, don't need 'em in the Gulch. I'm–'

'Look! Over there!' Dan interrupted him, pointing to the hill across Longhorn Gulch. The brightening dawn had revealed a group of riders poised on the hilltop. At the same moment Jack drew their attention to the end of Starlight Canyon where six men were taking up advantageous positions.

The sun rose above the hills filling the Gulch with warm light. The camp stirred and was suddenly galvanised into life when the crack of a rifle shot split the air. This signal set the group of riders into a gallop down the hillside to the Gulch. They split in two; one party hurled towards the herd whilst the other swung round the cattle and hit the camp before anyone knew what was happening. Wayman's cowboys scattered. Bullets spanged the air sending them diving for cover. The gunfire continued whilst Circle C cowboys drove the herd along the Gulch. Steers plunged and bellowed when they found a line of riders barring their way through the Gulch. They turned looking for some opening and found it in the entrance to the Canyon. Progress was slow but urged on by yelling cowhands the cattle were forced onwards. Dust rose above the bellowing steers pounding into the Canyon. When the last longhorn had disappeared from their view Brown's gunmen broke off the fight and sent their horses down the Gulch at a full gallop. Wayman's dust covered, dishevelled cowboys ran towards the Canyon but were sent diving dustwards by the six sentinels. Bullets cut the air as the two outfits flung lead at each other.

Wayman was the first to speak. 'Wal, I gotta hand it to Brown, he worked thet smoothly.'

Dan nodded. 'An' no-one could associate him with the rustlin'. I reckon them hombres thet attacked the camp were hired gunmen so thet no-one recognised them.'

Suddenly Frank started. He drew their attention to two cowboys who had detached themselves from Brown's outfit and were climbing the hillside.

'Reckon Brown wants to make sure none of your men try to git round 'em by comin' up here,' he said.

'C'm on,' Dan ordered. 'Time to git out of here.'

They hurried to their horses, leaped into the saddles and rode away from the hollow. Riding close to the Canyon rim they passed ahead of the slow-moving, seething mass of rustled cattle. The five riders halted and watched the sweating progress along the Canyon bottom and then mounted and rode again. All through the hot day it went on, riding and halting, riding and waiting, watching the herd driven onwards by the

Circle C cowpokes, urged along the floor of the canyon which rose gradually towards its head where it spilled over on to a huge expanse of plateau-like rolling grassland sloping gently away to the south and the border.

Whilst they pursued their grim determined course Dan and his companions could not help but admire the way in which Wes Brown handled his men and controlled the herd. His black clad figure was to be seen everywhere, urging, advising, commanding.

'A fine horseman and a fine cattleman,' commented Wayman. 'A pity he went the wrong side of the law.'

When they reached the rocky rim of the canyon Brown spread his men so as to control the cattle as they spilled on to the grassland. The longhorns spread out but were kept under perfect control by the dusty, sweating cowpunchers.

Dan held his four companions back until the herd was almost a speck on the horizon but as the sun reddened the darkening sky he closed the gap to keep the herd in view remaining at distance safe enough not to arouse suspicion.

Brown began to swing the herd towards a group of buildings and the steers were safely corralled before the darkness finally chased the light from the western sky.

Dan felt some sense of relief as the five cowboys proceeded cautiously towards the ranch. He had discovered where Brown brought rustled cattle but what next? His thoughts were interrupted by Wayman who called a halt.

'What do we do now?' he asked wiping his face. 'I'm figurin' on goin' in an' gettin' Brown.'

He was eager to get the rustler and get his cattle back. Dan laid a steadying hand on the rancher's arm.

'Not yet,' he said quietly. 'We're goin' to take a look around first. We'd be outnumbered if we went in there. This may only be a night stop so I want you to come with me whilst the others keep the horses ready.'

Wayman did not move. Suspicion mounted in his eyes. 'What you up to, McCoy? You could still pull a fast one. Shore you ain't in with Brown?'

Dan turned sharply in his saddle. His voice lashed Wayman like a whip. 'I don't like remarks like thet after what you've seen. I'm here to play out a theory I figured when I was sheriff and nothin's goin' to stop me 'cause I'm reckonin' on takin' up with Brown where I walked out three years ago.'

181

The tall cowboy swung his powerful frame out of the saddle and threw the reins to Frank. 'C'm on, Wayman, I want you with me jest in case I find anythin' interestin'.'

The rancher sat motionless. He grunted and slowly climbed out of the saddle. 'I don't git this. Why run any risk? We know Brown's rustled the cattle an' we know where they are so I figure we should high-tail it back, collect my boys an' see the cattle become mine again.' He stepped close to Dan, his eyes boring deep into the young cowboy. 'If you try anythin' when we git over there remember I'll not hesitate to use my Colt!'

Anger rose in Dan but he kept his temper. He ignored Wayman's threat. 'You'll git your cattle back.' His voice was cool and each word was stressed with deliberation. 'Now c'm on an' keep your eyes an' ears open.'

Chapter 12

Dan McCoy and John Wayman slowed their pace as the black silhouette of the ranch house loomed against the night sky. Keeping close to a fence they crept stealthily towards the long, low, wooden building.

A light shone from two windows and beyond light streamed from the bunkhouse where the cowboys showed obvious pleasure at having finished their job successfully.

Suddenly Dan froze in his step. A cowboy appeared at the door of the bunkhouse. He paused for a moment, looked across at the corrals, turned and disappeared.

Dan nodded to Wayman and the two men hurried silently across the space to the ranchhouse. Swiftly but stealthily they climbed the verandah rail and slunk into the shadows flattening themselves against the wall of the house. They paused for a moment until Dan signalled to his companion. Slowly they edged their way along the wall towards the lighted windows. They found the first one closed and the curtains drawn across it. Dan cursed their luck and silently hoped that the other was not the same. They slid across the wood and were relieved to hear voices drifting through the open window across which drawn curtains flapped in the slight breeze.

McCoy and Wayman sank low beside the window and Dan crept quickly to the opposite side so that each man covered the other should anyone appear to disturb their eavesdropping.

'Wal, Wes, you shore did wal to git those cattle through. I thought you'd lose quite a lot. It's a hard trail fer such a large herd. There'll be a big bonus in this fer you an' the boys.' There was satisfaction in the deep voice.

'It was pretty easy once we'd got rid of Wayman's horses,' replied Wes. 'There was little opposition especially as Wayman's bunch were tied up with the hired gunmen. You'll be payin' them off now?'

'Yeah. We won't need 'em fer a while yet. Wayman won't know who hit him; he'll hev to sell out now, an' cheap at thet – I'll certainly not offer what I did last time.'

Wayman, startled by this last remark, almost gave away their presence as he whispered 'Hiram Griffiths!'

'Thet'll give me some of the best ranchin' land in Texas an' extend the Circle C to the Brazo,' continued Griffiths. 'We can now turn our attention to the ranches north of Red Springs – git the land all round the town an' we'll control the town especially with Fennell in there as sheriff.' He spoke with obvious pleasure and satisfaction. 'We'll tackle the Bar Z next, Wes, but let this upheaval settle first, in the meantime scout out the possibilities.'

'Right, boss. When does this lot head fer the border?'

'We'll start changin' the brands tomorrow. Senor Ricardos will be here to take 'em in four days.'

Dan had heard enough. He was about to move away when the staccato sound of a hard ridden horse made him stop. The hoofs pounded the trail as if the devil pursued the rider. The conversation in the room stopped. A chair scraped the floor.

'Who can this be?' Griffiths voice was puzzled.

Footsteps approached the window. Quick as lightning Dan, with Wayman beside him, crossed the wood. They had just flattened themselves round the corner when the window was thrown further open.

'Can't see anyone yet,' said Griffiths, 'but he's shore in a hurry.'

The hoof beats drummed nearer. A rider lying flat along a horse's back appeared out of the darkness. McCoy and Wayman froze into the shadows of the verandah.

The light from the open window silhouetted Griffiths and the rider straightened in the saddle, pulling hard on the reins to bring his sweating mount to a dust whirling stop.

'Mr Griffiths!' shouted the rider. 'Wes Brown with you?'

'Yeah. What you want?'

The rider flung himself from the saddle and leaped on to the verandah as Brown joined his boss at the window.

'Zeke, what the hell's brought you down here?'

'McCoy, he's out of gaol!' panted the cowpoke.

'What!' The two men yelled together.

'Got out last night.'

'Damn Fennell. What's he done?' cursed Brown banging his fist on the window-sill.

'Let's hear his story first, Wes,' advised Griffiths.

'Come in, Zeke.'

As the two men stepped back into the room Zeke stepped over the window frame.

'This'll make them change their plans,' whispered Dan. 'C'm on let's hear 'em.'

They stole quietly along the verandah and peered cautiously through the window to see the dust-covered cowboy taking a drink from Griffiths.

'Thanks, Mr Griffiths. I shore need this.' He drained the glass in one gulp, replaced the glass on a tray and removed his dirt-stained sombrero.

Brown paced the floor impatiently. 'Now, Zeke, what happened?' His voice was agitated and his face clouded with annoyance.

'Wal boss, remember Butch an' his cronies were missin' from the Circle C when you left?'

Wes nodded.

'Seems they went after McCoy,' announced Zeke.

'What!'

'Yeah, an' it was a put up job with Fennell in it.'

Brown banged his fist on the table. 'The fool. What was he up to?'

Griffiths was more composed. 'Calm yourself, Wes; sit down. This may need more careful thinkin'. Go on, Zeke.'

'Sorry, boss,' apologised Brown taking a grip on his feelings as he sank into a chair.

'Seems like Barbara Collins stood Fennell up,' continued Zeke rubbing his hand across his dust-covered face. 'Fennell blew up at thet an' planned a little party fer McCoy.'

'What went wrong?' asked Griffiths.

'Two of McCoy's masked riders appeared jest as they were takin' McCoy out.'

'What!'

'Yeah, but guess what, boss. They were old man Collins and his son Howard.'

Brown sprang to his feet and even the poker-faced Griffiths looked startled.

'Knew it was someone local,' muttered Brown to himself.

'To the cut the story short,' went on Zeke, 'they reinstated Clint Schofield as temporary sheriff. He's there now with Bill Collins but there's no sign of McCoy, nor his brother, nor the two Collins boys.'

Wes looked puzzled. 'No idea where they are?'

'No.'

'How d'you learn all this?' asked Griffiths.

'I went into town jest after noon an' heard thet Collins had prevented the escape of McCoy an' thet Fennell was helpin' him to git out; wal, thet's what the townsfolk think happened. I thought I'd do a little investigation fer you so I tried to contact Fennell.

188

He wasn't in the cell with the outside wall but Jess Gordon was. He was with Butch an' the only one left alive. I contacted him through the window an' he told me the story. Thought you couldn't know fast enough so I grabbed a hoss an' high-tailed it out here as fast as I could.'

'Good work, Zeke,' commended Griffiths. 'Go an' grab yourself some grub.'

'Thanks, Mr Griffiths,' replied Zeke and crossed the room to the door.

McCoy and Wayman hastened round the corner. To Dan, impatient to overhear any conversation between Griffiths and Brown it seemed years before Zeke reached the bunkhouse. When they returned to the window Griffiths was speaking.

'Look here, Wes, I think you're seein' more in this than there really is.'

Brown, who was pacing the floor, swung round on Griffiths. 'McCoy was suspicious of us when he was sheriff. Why he didn't draw thet day I never figured. Somehow he got wind of our first rustlin' attempt otherwise why did he stampede the herd the way he did?' Brown raised his voice. 'An' thet's what he did, make no mistake about it. I turned it to our advantage an' Wayman thinks McCoy was tryin' to rustle.'

'Exactly, so Wayman'll think thet McCoy pulled this job when he hears McCoy's out of gaol. If he has wind of this place he couldn't attack us here – he hasn't sufficient men an' nobody'll believe him when they think he's escaped from gaol.'

Wes grunted his agreement. 'So what do we do?' he asked.

'Wal,' drawled Griffiths stroking his chin, 'we could jest carry on but with McCoy about an' someone believin' in him he's a menace. I'll hold up the movement of these cattle whilst you an' the boys git back to Red Springs. I figure he'll not be so far away an' he's shore to look fer you when he hears of this rustlin'. If you stir some trouble up in Red Springs – try to git Fennell out of gaol – you won't be long before you see McCoy an' a little reception party would finish things off.'

Wes grinned and slapped his thigh. 'It shore would.'

'We'll go to the sheriff's office an' demand an explanation about Fennell's arrest. When we show up Clint Schofield's shore to send word to McCoy an' we can prolong our stay until he arrives. You brief the boys an' arrange the set up. I'll be around to throw in a few words if necessary. You know I pride myself on bein' respected around Red Springs.' Griffiths laughed loud. 'Hev a drink, Wes, then warn the boys we ride early in the mornin' an' git a good night's sleep, there'll be a lot to do tomorrow.'

The two cowboys heard the whisky being poured out. They slipped quietly from the verandah and hurried towards the open grassland and their rendezvous with Frank, Jack and Howard.

As they rode across the expansive ranges towards the hills Dan related the results of the eavesdropping.

They dropped into a sheltered hollow and Dan called a halt.

'Reckon this'll do fer the night,' he said.

'Not stoppin' are we?' protested Wayman. 'I figure we should git back to Red Springs as soon as we can.'

Frank McCoy agreed with the rancher but the Collins boys were in favour of camping for the night.

'This thing's comin' right out into the open tomorrow so there's no need to sneak into Red Springs in the dark,' pointed out Jack.

'Jack's right,' said Dan. 'Besides we'd all be better fer a night's rest. We've got a good start on Brown an' we'll get started before sun-up.'

'But if we ride now,' argued Frank, 'we can git Mr Wayman's boys an' bush-wack this lot before they git to Red Springs.'

'Guess we could at thet,' smiled Dan, 'but thet will mean a lot of killin' an' the way I figure it there need hardly be any. Besides I want to take up with Wes in front of the townsfolk.'

'Right, son,' agreed Wayman swinging down from his horse. 'You've been on the mark all the way along.'

They soon had their camp ready and as they settled down Wayman looked curiously at Dan.

'What's your plan, son?'

'We'll pick up your cowhands an' be in Red Springs when the Circle C bunch git there.'

'An' a nice hot reception will be waitin' fer 'em,' grinned Frank.

'No,' asserted Dan. 'If all goes well I'm likely to be the only one to shoot but I'll give you the details in the morning.' Dan rolled himself in his blankets and was soon asleep.

Wayman glanced at the sleeping figure. 'I'm shore sorry fer the way I judged thet boy an' I'll see he's back as sheriff when this job's over, but I don't like the way he's stickin' his neck out.'

'He'll be all right,' said Frank. 'I'm stickin' close to him an' I'm keepin' my eyes peeled.'

The soft light of dawn was still missing from the eastern horizon when five cowboys climbed into their saddles and set out for Red Springs. Mile after mile they rode with their own thoughts; a silent, grim, determined bunch. By the time they reached the hills the Texas countryside had welcomed another day. Dan halted his horse, turned in the saddle and noted with satisfaction a cloud of dust on the horizon. With a curt, 'Here they come,' he urged his horse into a long steady lope. They dropped into Longhorn Gulch, kicked their horses into a gallop and soon covered the ground to Wayman's ranch.

The cowhands, questions pouring from their lips hurried forward to greet the five riders.

Wayman silenced them. 'We know where the cattle are an' we figure we'll hev the rustlers in Red Springs today. We hev no time to lose. Take your orders from Dan McCoy here an' git into the saddle quickly.'

Briefly but clearly Dan instructed the cowboys and within a quarter of an hour a determined bunch of men headed for Red Springs.

The town was a smudge on the horizon when Dan, Frank and the two Collins boys bade John Wayman goodbye and spurred their horses faster. They approached the town quickly but carefully and made their way through the side streets to the back of the gaol. They found the door locked but their knocking soon brought Bill Collins to the door.

'Who's there?' he called.

'Dan!' came the quick reply.

Eagerly Bill threw open the door to admit the four riders. He locked it behind them and followed them into the sheriff's office.

'You're back sooner than we expected,' said a surprised Clint jumping to his feet. 'Everythin' all right?'

'Yeah,' said Dan crossing to the window and peering out. The street was quiet and Texans went about their normal routine. 'The cattle are at Hiram Griffiths' place to the south awaitin' a move to the border.'

'Right, we'll raise a posse an' git 'em,' called Bill excitedly, striding towards the door.

'Hold it, Bill, the cattle will be all right. There's a little trouble brewin' here thet's got to be settled first. When thet's over Wayman can pick up the cattle at his leisure.'

Clint and Bill looked at each other, puzzled frowns marking their foreheads.

'Everythin's all right here,' grunted Clint. 'What goes, Dan?'

Before he answered Dan turned to Jack and Howard. 'Watch the back door jest in case.'

The brothers nodded and left the office.

'Frank, you keep a look out of thet window,' ordered Dan.

Frank moved obediently without a word and took his stand against the glass looking out on the main street. He took a rifle from the rack and eased his gun in its leather.

Dan smiled as he turned back to Clint and Bill. 'Don't look so worried, you two. I'll put you in the picture now.' Quickly he related the events since he left the gaol and of his plan to welcome Wes Brown.

The minutes ticked away in the clock on the wall in the sheriff's office, the tension mounting as the four men anxiously awaited the arrival of the Circle C outfit.

'Here comes Wayman,' called Frank, a slight tremor of excitement in his voice.

Dan was beside Clint in a flash. 'Right. Now Clint out with you when Wayman an' his boys pull up outside an' keep talkin' until Brown an' the Circle C git here. Bill, you go with him an' keep your eyes open.'

The two men grabbed their Stetsons and without a word obeyed the younger man.

The heavy sound of horses beat along the main street. They soon attracted attention and the word that 'Wayman's in town, there's been trouble,' spread like fire through the prairie grass. Red Springs crowded round the riders who had pulled up in front of the sheriff's office.

'What's wrong, Wayman?'

'Thought you were on the trail to the railhead, John?'

Questions were flying at the rancher as Clint and Bill stepped on to the sidewalk.

'Cattle rustled,' called Wayman. 'We were jumped out by Starlight Canyon. Where's Fennell?'

'Fennell's in gaol; mixed up with an escape bid by McCoy,' answered Clint. 'I've taken over temporarily.'

Wayman raised his eyebrows. 'Fennell an' McCoy? Wal, I haven't time to go into thet now. Reckon McCoy's gang still operates. We'd better hev a posse, Clint.'

'Hold it, John. Come inside an' let's hev the details; a small scoutin' party might be the wisest first.'

Wayman swung off his horse and strode

into the office. He smiled at Dan as he entered.

'Wal, Dan, all goes well so far. We've got an audience of townsfolk all we want now is Brown.'

The minutes ticked by. Frank reported that Wayman's cowboys were mixing with the crowd and were being eagerly questioned by the townsfolk. The minutes went by. The crowd was beginning to get restless wanting some action. A number of them started calling to Clint to hurry up. Wayman mopped his brow; Clint fingered his sombrero and Frank tensed himself as he peered along the street.

Dan looked worried. He wet his lips. He glanced sharply at his brother. 'Any sign yet, Frank?'

Frank shook his head.

'Maybe, Wes has altered his plan,' said Clint.

'He hasn't!' Frank yelled when he saw the Circle C riders pound into the main street. They reined the horses to a stop outside the sheriff's office. Clint and Wayman hurried to join Bill outside.

Dan moved close to the door. 'Right, Frank, keep tellin' me what's happenin'.'

'No one's moved off their horses yet.

Brown's talkin' to someone in the crowd. Circle C bunch droppin' out of the saddles one by one an' movin' amongst the crowd an' to various points along the street. Wayman's boys keepin' close to Brown's outfit as you told 'em.'

'Good,' whispered Dan.

'Brown dismounting! Movin' towards the office!'

'Right. Anyone gone in thet hotel?'

'Nope.'

'Quiet now.' Dan turned his attention to the voices outside.

'Hello, Wes,' called Wayman. 'Glad to see you. My cattle were rustled an' the bigger the posse we hev the better. We were jest leavin'.'

Brown halted at the foot of the two steps leading on to the sidewalk.

'Heard 'bout it,' replied Wes. 'Thought we might be of some help. Any idea who did it?'

'No. Can't be McCoy this time. He's still in there.' Wayman jerked his thumb towards the office behind him.

Brown was startled by this remark but outwardly he was composed.

'You shore?' he drawled.

'Certain.'

'You seen him?' Brown eyed Wayman suspiciously.

'Course I hev. First thing I checked on when I got into town. Your pal Fennell was helpin' him to escape but Collins here stopped it, clamped Fennell in gaol an' put Schofield in as temporary sheriff.'

Brown taken aback by the fact that Wayman had seen McCoy thought quickly.

'I suppose it could hev been McCoy's gang thet took your cattle. It would give 'em some hard ridin' but it would be possible an' maybe they'll use thet herd as a bargainin' fer McCoy.'

'Wal, let's git after 'em,' shouted Wayman, stepping on to the roadway.

'Hold it,' yelled Brown as the crowd shouted its approval.

'If it's McCoy's gang then he might hev some idea where they'd hole out. Let's hev him out an' make him talk.'

Shouts of approval came from the cowboys.

'Good idea,' said Wayman turning to Schofield. 'Bring him out Clint.'

The door of the sheriff's office opened and Dan stepped slowly outside. His eyes were sharp and his hands hung loosely by his side. The crowd gasped. Dan's footsteps echoed on the boards as he stepped forward.

'No need, Clint. I'm here!'

Silence struck the crowd.

Wes swung on Clint. 'What's the idea? What's he doin' out?' His voice was vicious.

'I'll do the talkin' Clint,' said Dan.

Clint and Bill stepped backwards on either side of the young cowboy.

'Guess you're surprised, Brown?' drawled Dan, his face grim.

'This is goin' to save a lot of trouble.' Brown's voice was cool as he collected his thoughts.

Dan noticed Wayman slip into the crowd and move close to the horseman who had ridden into town alone. Dan felt relieved; Wayman had Griffiths covered.

'It shore will,' said Dan quietly. He paused a moment then continued. 'Brown, there's a few things these here folk should know.'

The black dressed foreman from the Circle C looked Dan straight in the eyes. A grin flickered the corners of his mouth. 'Remember we stood like this three years ago McCoy an' remember what happened then,' mocked Brown.

Dan straightened at this remark. His lips tightened and his face lost its colour. 'Yeah, I remember,' he hissed, 'but there'll be a different endin' this time.'

'You bet there will,' lashed Brown. 'You'll not walk out this time. Instead you'll ride an' take us to that gang of yours.'

'Gang!' laughed Dan. 'I haven't any gang.' He raised his voice. 'Folks, the rustler stands in front of you now, an' his name is Wes Brown but–'

The crowd gasped.

'A good story,' yelled Brown. 'But you can't talk your way out of this one.'

'Can't I?' Dan's eyes narrowed. 'I'll tell you where Wayman's herd is at this moment.' He saw Brown start. 'It's on Hiram Griffiths' ranch over the hills to the south!'

Brown was shaken. He glanced round, nodded to his men. He saw them reach for their guns only to be stopped by Wayman's men before they ever touched them. Brown's face darkened as he looked back to Dan who replied:

'All your men are covered an' so is your boss over there.'

Brown spun round to see Griffiths turn to his horse only to find himself looking into the cold steel of a Colt in the hands of John Wayman.

'Wal, Brown,' drawled Dan, 'you may be convinced when I tell you that Wayman allowed you to take his cattle an' we trailed

201

you. I was outside thet window when Zeke arrived so I was able to plan this little reception fer you.'

Brown turned slowly to face Dan and Dan could not help but admire him. He was cornered and yet he was cool and collected. Dan felt sure that Brown still had something up his sleeve. He glanced swiftly at the hotel windows but saw no sign of a covering rifle. He had reckoned on seeing it. He could almost feel the eye lining him up with the sights. But which window? Dan could feel the sweat on his forehead. His hands felt clammy. No matter what, he had to play this out with Brown.

'Three years ago you called me yellow. Wal, Brown, the clock's back three years an' you an' I have to take up where we left off.'

A smile crossed the foreman's face. He shrugged his shoulders. 'All right if thet's the way you want it.'

Suddenly his hand flew to his Colt. It leaped into his hand and spat lead but Dan had been that fraction swifter. His Colt was in his hand blazing death into Brown's body as Dan flung himself to one side. A rifle crashed from somewhere behind him and as Dan hit the sidewalk he saw a body tip from a second-storey window of the hotel.

Dan picked himself up. Brown lay still at the foot of the steps. Frank stepped from the office door smoke still curling from his rifle.

'You all right, Dan?' he asked anxiously.

Dan slapped the dust from his clothes. 'Yeah. Thanks, Frank, thet was a mighty fine shot. I hadn't seen anyone up there.' He picked up his grey sombrero and rubbed it down.

'The cowpoke went in when you were takin' to Wes an' if the breeze hadn't moved a curtain I wouldn't hev known which window.'

Clint and Bill stepped forward to take the situation in hand as Wayman's men pushed the rustlers forward.

Dan turned and walked slowly along the sidewalk. Barbara stood against the rail. She smiled and held out her hands.

This Large Print Book, for people
who cannot read normal print,
is published under the auspices of

THE ULVERSCROFT FOUNDATION

... we hope you have enjoyed this book.
Please think for a moment about those
who have worse eyesight than you ...
and are unable to even read or enjoy
Large Print without great difficulty.

You can help them by sending a
donation, large or small, to:

**The Ulverscroft Foundation,
1, The Green, Bradgate Road,
Anstey, Leicestershire, LE7 7FU,
England.**
or request a copy of our brochure for
more details.

The Foundation will use all donations
to assist those people who are visually
impaired and need special attention
with medical research, diagnosis
and treatment.

Thank you very much for your help.